# BACK TO WHITECHAPEL

## LOVE THROUGHOUT TIME

### BOOK NINE

# ID JOHNSON

Copyright © 2025 by ID Johnson

All rights reserved.

No part of this book may be reproduced in any form or by any electronic or mechanical means, including information storage and retrieval systems, without written permission from the author, except for the use of brief quotations in a book review.

This is a work of fiction that blends historical elements with imaginative storytelling. While some names and events are drawn from history, the characters, actions, and interpretations presented here are fictional. Any resemblance to real persons, living or dead, is coincidental.

Cover by Sparrow Book Cover Designs

*For Polly, Annie, Elizabeth, Catherine, and Mary Jane. May you never be forgotten.*

# CONTENTS

# CARRIED AWAY

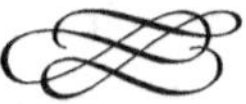



"London always smells like rain." I step onto the slick, uneven stones along the Thames River. As the tide slides out and leaves behind ribbons of mud and glinting debris, I crouch low to look for treasures. My boots stick slightly in the muck when I shift my weight. There's just something about this place. This river seems to remember everything that's happened along its shores for hundreds of years.

I promised myself I'd do something spontaneous when I finished my forensic psychology degree, and visiting my cousins in London felt like the perfect excuse for a trip. It's a graduation trip, technically, but mostly an escape from responsibility before I start my new job in New York City. So, my mom and I called her sister, my Aunt Claire, and planned the trip.

"Lena, you're ridiculous," my cousin Ella calls from behind me. "You do realize the tide comes in fast, right? You'll end up in the papers. *American Tourist Carried Away by River—While Looking for Trash.*"

I roll my eyes without looking up. "It's not trash. I've always wanted to go mud larking, actually, and this river is full of history, not trash."

My cousin Tom snorts. "You've watched one too many documentaries, and now you want to be an archaeologist."

I grin up at them. "Maybe I'm just better than my cousins at spotting things that matter. Plus, you two grew up here. Of course, it's not going to be as interesting to you as it is to me."

They're both standing on the embankment above me, holding paper cups of coffee like civilized people, while I'm knee-deep in muck with a trowel and a plastic bucket. I let Ella hold my phone and wallet so I don't ruin anything important.

"I can't believe this is the same river that ran through London at the same time Jack the Ripper was on his murdering spree," I call up. "It feels... calmer now."

"That's because you're not wading through it in 1888. Back then, it was basically a sewer. Whitechapel wasn't exactly riverside luxury," Tom says.

Ella agrees. "This part of the river isn't far from where the murders happened, though. Just north of here, on the East End. You can still feel the evil in some of the old alleys even though it's coffee shops, bookstores, and multi-cultural cuisines now instead of gin dens."

"So less murder, more lattes?"

"Exactly," Tom says, smirking. "Still dodgy in places, mind you. But these days it's mostly tourists and artists trying to make rent."

I glance at the water as it snakes past, steady and gray. "Crazy to think this same river's seen all of it. The ships, the smoke, the bodies...."

Ella shudders theatrically. "You really are leaning into the Ripper-tourist mindset, Lena."

"Maybe." I smile to myself. "But history and true crime have both always really intrigued me, and this place has both."

Last night's Jack the Ripper walking tour still lingers in my mind. We didn't see the whole East End, just the parts where a couple of the murders took place, but the stories are of women whose names I'll never forget–Mary Ann, Annie, Elizabeth, Catherine, and Mary Jane. There may have even been more....

Now, kneeling in the mud, that feeling intensifies. The river gurgles beside me, sliding back toward the sea, revealing the bones of the city one inch at a time.

I sift through silt with my gloved fingers, chasing a faint glint of something metal. It's probably just a bottle cap, but I keep scraping, heart thudding harder the more the shape reveals itself. First it's a curve, then a clasp, and I lift it out of the earth completely, exposing filigree work fine as lace.

When I rinse it in a puddle, I realize it's a small brooch the size of a silver dollar, dark with age but catching the light like it's been waiting for someone to notice it.

"Oh, my God," I shout.

"What?" Ella asks. "Did you find treasure?"

"Sort of." I hold it up so it shines in the sunlight. "See? I told you. I found a shiny piece of history."

Tom jumps down from the ledge to join me, squinting. "Let's see it, then." His boots instantly sink into the wet sand. "Ugh, this is disgusting."

"Careful," I warn, rinsing the brooch again. I notice this time that the back is engraved, delicate and worn but still legible: *Polly*. The name makes something flutter in my chest. "It says Polly. That was what they called Mary Ann Nichols," I say.

Tom frowns. "Who's that?"

"Weren't you listening last night? She's one of Jack the Ripper's victims," I explain, barely able to hide my excitement. "She was killed not far from here, actually. The tour guide mentioned it."

Ella groans. "You've officially lost your marbles."

"Marbles or not, this is real." I beam, brushing off the last of the dirt. "The Ripper might have dropped it."

"Or maybe," Tom cuts in, "it's just a random old brooch from a junk shop that ended up in the river with a common name. It's a complete coincidence."

I ignore him and fasten it to my shirt, just below my collarbone. One needs a license to mudlark in the Thames. I begged my aunt to get one before I came. Now, it's paying off. Technically, I'm not allowed to take anything out of the country when I go, but I can wear it for now. "See? It's beautiful, and I rescued it."

"Oh, great. Now I'm stuck." Tom puts his hand on my shoulder, trying to get his boot out of the sludge.

Under his weight, I slip on the wet stones. In an instant, I lose my balance. The ground gives way beneath me, crumbling into thick, sucking mud.

"Lena!" Ella shrieks.

The sky spins, and cold water slaps against my legs, waist and chest, faster than I can comprehend. It feels like the river is rising, and I reach for Tom's hand, his shirt, anything, but the river tugs at me like it's alive.

"Grab her!" Ella screams.

Tom tries to grab me, and I grasp his wrist, but then the tide surges higher, dragging me backward with a powerful determination to pull me under. I lose my grip as the shock of cold knocks the breath from my lungs.

The current is relentless. My boots are heavy. I can't tell which way is up. Everything turns to gray and blue-green, all other sounds swallowed by the rush of water. I part my lips to scream, and the river fills my mouth, icy, ancient, and angry.

I thrash, panicking. The surface flashes above me, light and air, and then it's gone again, replaced by the murky dark. I can't see. I can't breathe. My lungs burn, the pressure building until stars explode behind my eyes.

Something brushes my arm, a coil of riverweed, or maybe a hand. My heart hammers so hard it hurts my chest. The water roars in my ears, louder than the city ever was, a deep, guttural groan.

I reach up, but my limbs are slow, heavy, and sluggish. The current pulls harder, wrapping around me like chains. My chest convulses, the need for air turning into a blazing fire. Every instinct screams to fight, but it's like the river doesn't want to let me go.

My vision tunnels. Light shatters above, rippling like a broken mirror. For a fleeting second, I swear I hear someone calling for me, faint and far away, ripping through the dark water.

Then the sound fades. The pressure fades. Everything fades.

The last thing I feel is the weight of the river closing over me, cold and endless. Then there is only darkness.

# NO ONE DESERVES THIS

*MARK*

Fog swallows the light whole tonight, rolling through the alleys of Whitechapel. I run hard, my boots splashing through puddles, my coat snapping behind me as I blow my whistle.

The man ahead of me is nothing but a shifting shadow in the haze. He darts left, the glint of a knife in his hand briefly catching the street light before vanishing again.

"Stop!" My voice is hoarse and useless.

I only hear the echo of his flight, the slap of boots on stone, the frantic rasp of my lungs.

I round the corner and nearly skid into the wall of mist that hangs over the Thames embankment, and I lose sight of him entirely.

"Bloody hell," I hiss, scanning the shadows. The bank is empty. I ball my hands into fists, adrenaline twisting into fury. I had him. I *had* him—

Then I hear another woman scream, but this time it's coming from the water. The surface heaves and shifts under the dim light, and then I see her arms flailing, her hands clawing before slipping back under.

"Blast!" I shrug off my coat and jump in the river, kicking hard, following the swirl of bubbles downward. The current drags at me, tearing at my clothes, my limbs, my strength.

Fingers brush mine, and I grab hold, pulling her upward, the weight of her dragging at my shoulders. Her body is limp. I break the surface with a gasp, hauling her toward the bank, every stroke a battle against the tide.

"Hold on," I mutter, though she can't hear me. "You're not dying tonight, not if I can help it."

When I finally reach the embankment, I hook my arms under hers and drag her out of the water. She collapses against me, coughing, water pouring from her mouth. Her face is the palest white, her lips blue, and her clothes are soaked through… and quite odd.

"Easy," I say, forcing breath into my lungs. "You're safe now."

She coughs up more water, gasping for air. I retrieve my coat and drape it around her shoulders, squatting beside her. Her blonde hair is plastered to her face, but her skin is smooth and unscarred. There's no sign she was attacked before falling.

"Are you well?" I ask. My voice is steadier than I feel. "Did you see a man with a knife run through here? Did he push you into the river?"

She coughs, struggling to get words out through choked lungs. "What? No, I didn't see a man," she says.

Her accent is unfamiliar, not Cockney, not proper London, but something else entirely.

I glance down at her clothes: men's trousers and a loose men's shirt. "Where were you going tonight, miss?"

When she catches her breath, she looks up at me. "I… I'm visiting family here. In London. I—my name's Lena. Lena… uh… Carter."

"Visiting from where, miss?"

"From New York." Her voice wavers. "Where're my cousins?"

I look around, but there's no one else here. "I see no one, miss."

She sits up then, blinks a few times, and looks around, pulling my jacket close to her. In my wet state, I wish I had it back, but she needs it more than I do. "Where are we?"

"Whitechapel," I reply, studying her face. "Do you require a physician?"

"When are we?" Her forehead puckers. I don't understand her question, but she seems to be speaking to herself anyway. Her eyes meet mine, and she tips her head to the side. "Can you help me find them? Perhaps they're planning on meeting me at the tavern."

The thought of leaving her alone in Whitechapel makes my gut twist. The streets are dark, but I have duties elsewhere. I can't stick around to protect her. I can only get her somewhere safe.

"I'll see you to the tavern," I say, helping her to her feet.

The streets are eerily quiet now. Her eyes dart at every shadow, and I sense the source of her unease is more than having fallen into the river. She studies everything around her, and I wonder if she's frightened–or mad.

We reach the Ten Bells, the closest tavern to where I found her. Tucked in a side alley, its sign swings and creaks above the door, and through the window I can see the fair redhead who tends the bar. Inside, it smells of burning peat and ale. Miss Carter hesitates on the threshold.

"My family's meeting me here," she says, clutching my coat tighter around her shoulders. "They'll take care of me now. Thank you for your help."

I nod reluctantly. "Wait here, then. Don't leave without your family."

She gives me my coat back, a grateful smile on her face. Then she slips inside, and I go back to work.

The woman I left behind on the street, the one with her throat slit, is still out there. Her body waits, and so does justice. I put my coat on, still soaked to the bone. But the shiver that passes through me isn't from cold, but from the knowledge that a killer walks free.

When I arrive, the body still rests in the same place in the alley where I left her. I lift my whistle to my lips and blow a sharp, commanding note. Soon, a constable arrives, his lantern bobbing.

"Inspector Harrow, sir," he says.

"Post men at either end of the street," I order, gesturing to the entrances. "Don't let anyone through. Get word to the station to send for the chief inspector and the coroner. Tell them to hurry. This woman was attacked and brutally murdered"

He nods and runs to comply. I kneel beside the woman's body, careful not to touch more than necessary until the others arrive. The cut to her throat is deep, clean, and precise. Smaller, shallow stabs line her lower abdomen. I pull my notebook out of my coat pocket, thankful that it's dry, and note everything–the position of the body, clothing, approximate age, apparent health, and all injuries.

The alley is littered with debris–broken bottles, fragments of wood, footprints that have mostly faded on the wet stones. I sketch the scene roughly, marking distance from lamplight posts, puddles, and objects near the body. Every scrap could prove useful later. Most detectives wouldn't bother, but I've found such notes helpful in other cases, and something tells me this one is bigger than any other.

Another constable arrives, and I assign him to one side of the alley, stationing the one who left to fetch him at the other. "No touching and no moving of anything until Chief Abberline arrives," I instruct them. "Understand?"

He nods, tension visible in every line of his body.

I rise, pacing the scene. The gaslight barely covers the walls and windows of the nearest buildings. Shadows swallow up this part of the street; I'd be shocked if anyone saw anything at all.

I call out to any early risers nearby, dockhands, street vendors, shopkeepers, asking if they saw or heard anything unusual. Everyone shakes their heads as though the night passed quietly. Still, I record each statement meticulously.

Finally, I return to the woman's body one last time, committing her to memory. I don't yet know her name, her story, or why she was here alone. I only know the facts I can gather tonight: the attack was sudden, carried out swiftly, and no one saw anything. No one other than me even heard anything. I heard her screams, but I arrived too late to see the attack.

The coroner's wagon arrives just as dawn seeps into the sky, orange light spilling over the alley. I step back as the men lift her body onto the stretcher, covering her face with a sheet. The sound of the fabric settling hits harder than usual.

"She didn't deserve this, no matter who she was," one of them says.

"No one deserves this. This is gruesome, even for Whitechapel," another responds.

I glance once more at the ground where she fell. The blood settles into uneven pools. I don't need a coroner to tell me what she did for a living. She was one of the countless women who haunt these streets after midnight, trading their bodies for enough coin to keep the cold out for one more night. Desperation will make people do just about anything.

I stare down the alley toward the glowing river brume. "God help us," I mutter under my breath.

Whitechapel: the rot, the poverty, the gin houses spilling their drunks into the gutters, and the lodging packed twelve to a room. I've walked these streets for years, and the filth multiplies with each passing day. No law holds here for long. Hunger and filth grind it down to dust. I can haul a thief in on Monday and see him back at his old trade by Wednesday, laughing in my face.

I've seen men gutted for a shilling, children starving, and women who vanish without a trace, but this feels different. The precision and location of the cuts on her body make it feel personal.

I turn my collar up and start walking toward the station. Behind me, the river splashes against the embankment, carrying secrets downstream.

# THE TEN BELLS

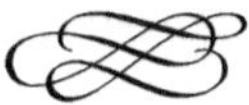

## *LENA*

I PUSH open the tavern door, and warmth washes over me. My jeans cling to my legs, my soaked shirt sticks to my chest, and a shiver rolls down my spine. I move toward the bar, trying not to look too out of place, my boots squeaking against the wooden floor.

"You look like you've had a rough night," a voice says, calm but curious.

I look up to see a woman leaning on the counter, her red curls spilling over her shoulders, setting off her bright blue eyes. She tilts her head, studying me.

"I… I fell into the river," I manage, my voice trembling.

She nods once, a faint smile tugging at her lips. "You sure did," she says. "My name's Shannon Connor. Sit down, warm yourself. You're soaked to the bone."

I slide onto a nearby stool. "I'm Lena," I say, my teeth chattering. I fold my wet hands in my lap, suddenly aware of how out of place I am. How in the world did I end up here? "I didn't mean to cause any trouble."

"Trouble?" Shannon repeats lightly, amusement in her tone. "You've already had enough of that tonight, I'd say."

I manage a small, tired laugh and glance around, trying to figure out what time period I've stumbled into. I know I'm not where I should be. Like the rest of the city I'd seen on the way here, this place is archaic, while somehow still… new.

"Can I ask what the date is?" I force my voice to sound casual. My stomach churns, and I curl my fingers around the damp fabric of my shirt.

Shannon gestures to a smoke-stained wall calendar. "Thirty-first of August," she says plainly.

I look at the calendar and freeze. *August 31, 1888.* This can't be possible. I fell into the river… and back through time?

Maybe I'm in a hospital somewhere–in a coma. Maybe I'm dead…

Memories from the Jack the Ripper tour flare in my mind. The stories, the streets, and the first murder, which will take place tonight. Unless he's already killed her.

Maybe this is hell.

Shannon looks me over again more closely this time. "You're not from around here, are you?"

"No," I admit, my voice careful. It all seems real. I need to play along until I can figure out what happened. "I'm from New York."

"Do you have anywhere to stay tonight? Or any dry clothes?"

I shake my head. "No. I don't. I can't seem to find my cousins."

"Then come with me." She motions to the stairway behind the bar. "I've got a room upstairs. It's small, but it's safe and dry. You can change there, and there's an extra bed to sleep in."

I follow her up the narrow, creaking stairs, each step reminding me that I'm far from home, far from everything familiar. The city noise drifts in through the walls–but it's carriage wheels, horses' hoofs, not the roar of engines. Every sound is foreign, every detail jarring.

This was supposed to be a fun trip. It was supposed to be a week in London with Tom and Ella, celebrating before starting my new job doing criminal profiling with the New York City Police Department. I'm supposed to be visiting museums and old pubs right now, not dripping on the floor of one in 1888.

Shannon opens a door at the top of the stairs. The room is small, with cracked walls and four small beds tucked into the corners. A tiny trunk sits at the foot of one of the beds, and the air smells of sweat, unwashed linens, and smoke. The window lets in a sliver of light from the lamp-lit street below.

I glance around, noticing the faint sound of laughter and muffled voices from down the hall, the soft rustle of skirts and the clink of bottles. A ribbon of lace spills from a trunk, and a corset hangs over the back of one bed. The musky scent of sex in the air hits me, and it's only then that I realize this isn't just a boarding house above a bar. This is a brothel. A mix of disbelief and unease falls over me, and yet, I'm grateful for Shannon and her kindness. I could be walking the streets now—freezing, lost, and confused.

She sets a bundle of clothing on the nearest bed. "Here." She tucks a stray curl behind her ear. "Change into these. They should fit."

I pull back the folds and find a simple nightgown and a pair of dry wool socks.

"Go on, change," she says softly. "I have to get back downstairs."

After I thank her, she returns to her work. I slip out of my wet clothes and pull on the dry garments. The fabric scratches my skin, but it's warm and dry. I tug on the stockings, pin the *Polly* brooch to the nightgown, and finally sit on the edge of the bed, hugging my knees.

I glance around the small room, taking in the thin blankets on the bed, the lingerie and whiskey bottles strewn about. The smell of the room makes me wrinkle my nose, but I am alive, dry, and out of the river.

Curling up on the bed, I try to hold on to the small thread of security this room provides. My mind spins with the date, the streets outside, and the reality that I am somewhere I've only ever read and heard tales about. I am in 1888, in Whitechapel, London, and nothing makes sense.

My limbs ache from fighting with the river, and I'm beyond tired, despite the fact that it was only late afternoon when I fell into the water. I tuck the blanket around my shoulders, lying on my side facing the door, and try to quiet my thoughts, but the image of the man in uniform flashes through my mind.

I didn't tell him the truth. I said I was meeting family, which, of course, is a lie. I'd suspected as soon as I saw his uniform and looked around that this was an entirely different time, but if I'd told him that, he would have thought I'd lost my mind. Who knows what he would have done? He would've thought me mad or drunk. He would've locked me in jail or an asylum.

My eyelids grow heavy, and my thoughts scatter. Somewhere between the rhythm of my heartbeat and the distant sounds of the tavern, I fall asleep.

When I awaken, it's not the soft morning light I expect to greet me. Instead, I hear the low murmur of voices and the shuffle of movement in the room. I open my eyes, and for a moment, all the disorientation returns in a rush. I sit up and try to adjust my eyes against the lantern glow while taking in the figures entering the room.

Shannon appears first, carrying the lantern. Behind her come two other women. Their clothing is layered and worn: bodices cinched over faded skirts, underskirts peeking from beneath, stockings patched in places. The scent of alcohol, smoke, sweat, and perfume hangs around them. They move with an ease and confidence that tells me they know this life well.

Shannon tilts her head, giving me a faint, amused smile. "You awake, then?" she asks.

I nod, trying to pull myself together. "I am." My voice sounds small and fragile.

She gestures toward the other women. "These are Louisa and Flossie. They share this room with me."

Louisa, a dark-haired woman with red rouge on her cheeks and crimson lipstick, steps forward. Her bodice is slightly askew. She offers a nod. "Good evening," she says simply.

Flossie, a tall blonde, follows, her gaze meeting mine, and she smiles faintly, the corners of her eyes crinkling. "Nice to meet you."

I manage a weak smile in return. "My name is Lena," I choke out awkwardly.

Shannon plops down on her bed. "It's nearly dawn. We just got done with work. We keep strange hours around here. You'll see," she says with a wink.

I sit on the edge of the flimsy mattress, watching them get ready for bed, noticing the details: the small hooks for hanging skirts, the brass buckles on their shoes, the scent of lye soap. I see their frayed hems and carefully hidden stains. Their garments are meant to be seen by many and touched by the hands of strangers. The layers, the tight fit, the fabrics tell me everything I need to know: these women work beneath the shadows of the night, and it's a world in which I never thought I'd ever even catch a glimpse.

"What kind of work do you do, Lena?" Flossie asks.

I swallow hard, my throat dry. I hadn't thought about work yet, but now, looking around the room, I realize that if I'm going to stay here, I can't just lie in bed and wait for someone else to care for me. This place isn't a charity, and I have no money, no contacts, and no plan.

"I could serve drinks," I say. "I can help in the tavern downstairs."

Flossie nods, and Shannon chuckles. "Well, that's practical. We can always use another hand behind the bar. You'll learn fast enough. You won't make as much coin as we do, but it'll be enough to pay for your bed."

Relief mingled with apprehension floods me. It isn't glamorous or even safe, but it's a start. I nod, more determined than I feel. "Thank you."

Shannon smiles. "Good. We'll get you settled and show you the ropes. Welcome to the Ten Bells, Lena."

*Ten Bells.* I know this place. I just walked these floors on a tour, tracing the footsteps of Jack the Ripper's victims. This very building is one of the most infamous stops on the true crime map of Whitechapel. I can't believe I didn't recognize it, and now, I'm sitting here, watching these women, Louisa, Flossie, and Shannon, and a knot tightens in my stomach. They are very exposed, and their lives are incredibly dangerous.

The stories weren't just stories. The terror was... *is* real, and somehow I'm caught in the middle of it. I should be back with my cousins, my aunt and uncle, and my mom, spending our trip laughing over tea and pastries. I already miss them, and picturing them believing I've drowned in the Thames twists a cold panic through me.

# RUMORS

## *MARK*

THE CORONER'S office reeks of blood. As I stand near the slab, I pull the sheet back just enough to glimpse her face: pale, still, the life drained from her. The slit of her throat causes my stomach to churn. I've seen many dead bodies, but nothing this violent before. Whoever did this was filled with rage and cruel intentions.

I step away, knowing I can't identify her alone, and set out to find my childhood friend, Nellie. We grew up together in the nearby town of Surrey. Nellie came from a destitute family, and like so many of the girls we knew, she took to the streets of London to survive. I've tried to get her work elsewhere, but she insists she doesn't need my help or anyone else's.

This morning, I find her exactly where I expect, on the corner of Osborn Street and Brick Lane. She sees me coming and greets me with a nod and a smile.

"Nellie," I murmur, keeping my voice low. "I need you to come with me. There's a body at the coroner's, and I need you to tell me if you recognize her."

She hesitates for a moment and glances toward the alley, wary of being seen with a cop, then follows.

At the coroner's office, I guide her to the deceased. I pull the sheet back slightly, letting her see, and she gasps. Then she swallows and whispers the name I've been hunting for.

"Polly Nichols," she sniffles.

*This is not just another body. This is a woman, and she had a life. Her name was Polly.*

"Thank you, Nellie. I'm sure that must've been difficult. Did you know her well?" I ask, covering the body with the sheet.

"Yes. She was a good friend. A right good woman," Nellie says, tears rolling down her cheeks. "She'd never hurt anyone. Not a soul. Went by Polly, but her real name is Mary Ann. Sad thing is, she's got five children."

The name changes everything. The investigation begins in earnest now, and I can already feel the web of clues threading through these miserable streets. Now, I have something concrete, a foothold for the investigation. Every alley, every doorway in Whitechapel suddenly becomes a place to probe, to follow the trail left by whoever committed this terrible act.

I place a hand lightly on Nellie's shoulder. "That's enough for now. Thank you," I say. She nods, wiping away tears, and I guide her to the door.

"Be careful," I add, though she doesn't need the warning; surviving Whitechapel has taught her every way to dodge danger. She gives me one last nod and then melts into the crowd.

My mind won't stop turning over the case, but as I try to focus on the facts, another image keeps creeping in: the American woman I pulled from the Thames last night, the one wearing men's clothes, soaked and nearly drowning in the river. Lena, she said. Something about her unsettles me.

The timing of the damsel in distress was nothing short of impossible. Or did she *pretend* to fall in the river to throw me off the trail of whoever killed Polly? Perhaps they were working together? And why the men's clothes? It gnaws at me, a suspicion I can't shake.

By evening, I find myself back at The Ten Bells. The door swings open, and I'm surprised to see Lena behind the bar. Someone, one of the ladies of the night, no doubt, has dressed her in a corset, brushed her golden hair into soft waves, and touched her cheeks with rouge. Somehow, even like this, she doesn't look like the women around her. She still seems wholesome and elegant in a way that makes her stand apart from the tavern's usual patrons.

I shake off the thought. There is no room for admiration or distraction. I step up to the bar. "Miss Carter?" I begin.

Her eyes meet mine, wide and startled. For a moment, she doesn't move, as if weighing whether to run or stay. I can see the hesitation and uncertainty in her expression and posture. She swallows hard, then speaks. "It's good to see you again. I never got your name or a chance to thank you properly for saving me."

"I was just doing my job, miss. No need to thank me. My name is Inspector Mark Harrow. I was hoping to ask you a few questions about last night. Could you please join me for a brief meeting at the station house?"

She pauses, her hand lingering on the edge of the bar. After a moment, she exhales and nods. She says something to one of the other women working behind the bar and walks around the corner. I fall in step beside her, careful not to crowd her as we leave the tavern behind.

Inside my office, I close the door behind us as Lena's eyes dart around the room. She perches on the edge of a chair, her hands folded tightly in her lap. I take a seat across from her, and the silence stretches for a moment, letting her settle while I organize my thoughts.

"Tell me," I begin carefully. "Why were you dressed as a man last night?"

"I was trying to pass as a man while I walked," she admits. "I didn't want trouble. You know, I just didn't want some brute to take advantage of me. It seems safer to pretend to be a man in order to not be harmed by men."

I nod, letting the explanation settle. If it's a lie, it's a very clever one.

"And why work at the tavern now? You said your family was going to meet you here."

"My family never showed up, and I needed a job to earn my keep and stay in the room above the tavern."

"Do you know anything about what happened last night? About the woman who was found dead?"

"With all due respect, I know more than you do, Inspector."

My brow lifts. "Is that so?" I lean forward slightly, my curiosity piqued. "Tell me what you know."

She swallows, glancing briefly at the door as if measuring how much she can say. "Mary Ann Nichols. Buck's Row. She was in a pool of blood with her throat cut and five or six stab wounds to her gut."

I keep my expression and tone neutral, though I can't believe my ears.. "How do you know that?"

"Rumors," she says. "The streets talk, Inspector."

I nod, though I'm trying to calculate whether or not she's lying. Alas, how else would she know?

"Am I free to go back to work now, sir?"

She looks at me with hope in her pretty blue eyes, and I feel the tug of wanting to keep her here. I quickly shove those feelings away.

"You may go."

She rises gracefully, adjusting the folds of her dress, still wary but composed. "Thank you, Inspector, and thank you again for pulling me out of the river. I don't know how I can repay you."

"You can repay me by keeping an eye out and keeping yourself safe," I say. I walk her back to The Ten Bells, knowing the streets of Whitechapel at night are no place for her alone. She keeps pace beside me, quiet yet alert, her arms tucked around her body as she still has no coat.

When we reach the door, I hesitate for a fraction of a moment, taking in her strikingly beautiful face. Her confidence and the sharp intelligence in her eyes, especially here, in the trappings of the tavern, are remarkable, and unlike any woman I've ever met.

"Stay safe," I tell her once more, offering a final nod before turning away.

How could she possibly know so much about the deceased, every gruesome detail of her death, without having been there? Were her answers a product of the rumor mill, or was she an accomplice? An uneasy feeling tightens in my gut. Whoever she is, whatever her intentions, she has stepped into this case in a way I can't ignore.

And now, I have to find out everything I can about Mary Ann Nichols–and Lena Carter.

# DANGEROUS OBSESSION

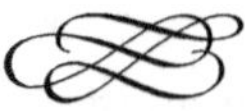

## *LENA*

I WAKE up to the afternoon sun pouring through the window. Flossie is already sitting up, humming to herself as she braids her hair. Louisa snores softly in the next bed, her arm thrown over her face, while Shannon tugs at the laces of her worn corset, muttering about how it's shrinking by the day. I lie still for a moment, listening to the floorboards creak beneath her feet, and try to quiet my mind, but it won't be quiet, not after last night.

Even now, I find myself analyzing, noting patterns and inconsistencies the way I learned to do in my training. It's automatic, a habit I can't switch off, even in a foreign city and a totally different century.

The handsome Inspector Mark Harrow's face keeps rising behind my eyelids. I remember the way he looked at me when I spoke about Polly Nichols. It was as though he was holding back what he truly wanted to say. I shouldn't have said so much. He asked questions in a calm, professional manner, and I answered because I wanted to help. Maybe if he knows I'm paying attention to the case, he'll let me help prevent the next murder. I would focus on details, on what the scene can tell us about the killer's habits and mindset. It's the kind of thinking I've been taught to do. I've spent the last four years learning criminal profiling, connecting evidence, and anticipating behavior.

"Lena, are you awake?" Shannon calls, fastening her skirt. "We've got to get downstairs before George starts hollerin'."

"I'm up," I mumble, swinging my legs out of bed and dressing quickly, keeping my back to the others, my thoughts still circling Harrow's questions.

By the time we head down to the tavern, Shannon is already chatting about the night ahead, about some musician coming in, the promise of good crowds, a chance for decent tips, but I barely hear her. I pick up a rag and begin wiping the counter.

"Cheer up, love," Shannon says with a grin. "It's Friday. Could be a good night."

I glance toward the door. Jack the Ripper is still out there somewhere. Walking. Breathing. Watching. He's most certainly already been in this tavern, laughing with the girls and drinking from these very cups. The thought gives me goosebumps.

If I can help Harrow find him, I will. Even if it means putting myself in danger. Even if it means he learns just how much I really know.

By nightfall, The Ten Bells is bursting at the seams. The fiddler in the corner plays a lively tune while tankards slam against tables. Men shout for more ale, slap girls on their bottoms, and call each other names in accents from every corner of London and beyond. The lamps burn low, the brass fittings sticky from a day's worth of spilled drink, and the floor is slick under my boots.

I'm weaving through the crowd with a tray balanced on my palm when Shannon calls out, waving me over to the bar. "Lena! Come meet these lovely ladies, just in for a drink before work."

The two women she's with both smile, open and genuine, the kind of smiles that make me like them right away. Annie has sandy-brown curls and a round, pleasant face. I remember her from a photograph I saw on the Ripper tour, and the realization slams into me so hard my stomach twists. *No! It can't be!* But the more I look at her, the more certain I am. She's Annie Chapman.

Next, I look at the taller woman beside her. She has pretty blue eyes, strawberry-blonde hair, and an hourglass figure, exactly like the stories described. I try not to look as startled as I am.

"Lena, this is Annie," Shannon says. "And this is Mary Jane."

"Good evening," I somehow manage to say, setting down the tray.

"Evenin' yourself," Mary Jane answers with a soft Irish lilt. "You new here?"

"Yes. Very new," I say, and she nods, the sort of nod that says she knows what it means to start over.

Annie takes a sip of gin. "You live upstairs, then? Shannon said you are stayin' with her?"

"That's right."

"We was just saying how it'd be nice to have steady work indoors," Mary Jane says. "No men sweatin' all over you. No coppers sniffin' 'round."

The sounds of the tavern dim for a heartbeat–the laughter, the fiddler, the clatter of mugs. It's all still there, but it feels far away. *Annie Chapman. Mary Jane Kelly.* I want to tell them to leave London, to hide, to never walk the streets of Whitechapel again.

Instead, I swallow hard. "You'll both be careful tonight, won't you? Things haven't been safe here lately."

Mary Jane gives a sad smile. "They're never safe for lassies like us, but what can we do? We can't *eat* careful."

Annie nods. "Every night is a risk. We just hope this night's kind."

The fiddler picks up a quicker tune, and the men grow even more rowdy. Somewhere behind me, someone starts singing loudly and off-key.

An hour later, I spot Annie near the door, talking with a man in a dark coat. His face is lost beneath his hat brim. He says something that makes her throw her head back and laugh, then she looks toward the door.

I want to stop her. I take one step forward, but Shannon's calling for help with a tray of mugs, and by the time I look again, Annie's gone.

The music plays on, the laughter rolls over it, and I keep wiping the counter because if I stop, I'll start shaking.

When the rush slows and only a few stragglers linger over their drinks, I can't shake the image of Annie's face or the way she smiled before leaving. I glance toward the door for the hundredth time, hoping to see her come back, but she doesn't. The musician packs up, Shannon and I wash the last of the mugs, and the air begins to clear of smoke and noise.

"Shannon," I say quietly.

She looks up from the rag in her hand. "What's got you looking so pale, love? You see a ghost?"

"Not yet," I say, trying to sound light, but my voice shakes. "Do you know where I can find Inspector Harrow?"

She looks at me with disgust. "Harrow? The copper?"

I nod.

"Why in the hell would you want to talk to a copper?" she asks, lowering her voice. "You trying to get yourself in trouble? We don't go seeking out their company, Lena. They come sticking their noses in our business enough as it is."

"It's important," I say. "I just need to speak with him. Please, Shannon."

She stares at me like I've lost my mind. "You mean to say you'd go out there, in the middle of the night, hunting down a bobby?"

"I don't want to go wandering around looking for him," I admit. "But I will if I have to."

She sighs, rubbing the back of her neck. "Sometimes, I hear he takes a pint down at the Blind Beggar, just a few blocks over. It's a quiet spot."

"Thank you," I whisper, already reaching for the shawl I borrowed from Flossie.

The streets are almost empty when I step outside. Somewhere in the distance, a man laughs way too loudly, and I pull the shawl tighter as though it'll protect me. The streets are so much darker when barely lit by gas lamps. No wonder no one ever saw the killer. Every shadow looks like it's hiding someone. Every turn of the alley feels like walking into a story I already know the ending to.

*Jack the Ripper.* He doesn't have that name yet, but I know it all the same. He's real, alive, and somewhere in this maze of streets.

By the time I spot The Blind Beggar, my heart is pounding. The place is small with a single candle glowing in the window. Inside, only a handful of men sit at tables with their drinks, and there, at the end of the bar, is Inspector Harrow.

He's leaning over a half-empty glass, reading something folded in his hands. When he glances up and sees me, surprise spreads over his face.

"Miss Carter," he says, standing. "You shouldn't be out alone at this hour."

"I needed to talk to you," I say, my voice shaking.

He gestures for me to sit, and I do, feeling the warmth of his tone chase away a sliver of my nervous energy. I want to tell him everything: that Annie Chapman will be dead in a month, that Mary Jane Kelly won't live to see mid-November, but the words stick in my throat. How could I explain? How could he possibly believe me? So instead, I talk about crime scenes and forensics.

I begin cautiously. "About Polly Nichols and the place where she was found. It struck me that there's so much that could be done to preserve evidence, even the simplest things."

Harrow leans forward. "Evidence? We collected what we could, but—"

"I know," I interrupt meekly, "but sometimes evidence gets mishandled, even without meaning to. Fingerprints, for instance. If someone touches a weapon, a railing, even the ground nearby, you can lift impressions. Even the killer's boots might have left prints in the blood. Right now, you're relying on witness statements, but the physical traces could tell you so much more."

His eyes fill with curiosity. "Fingerprints? I've heard talk of it, but—"

"You don't need anything fancy," I say quickly. "Something as simple as coating the surface with chalk, dusting lightly, then carefully lifting it with paper. You might not catch everything, but you'd know more with any fingerprints you can lift from the scene because everyone's fingerprints are different, you see?"

I lift my finger, letting him see the delicate swirl of lines etched into my skin. Then I take his hand gently, showing how his index finger is different than mine. When our fingers brush, a spark of electricity spreads between us, startling in its intensity.

I let go of his hand and clear my throat, trying to keep my train of thought. "And the boot prints in the alley, they get washed away or trampled before anyone notes them. Even small bits of blood, preserved carefully, could tell you the direction he came from, how much he weighs, and how the victim was moved. It's all in the details, if someone takes the time to note them correctly."

He swallows, staring down at his glass as though seeing the crime scenes again in his mind. "And the constables, they don't always know to take such care," he mutters.

"Exactly," I say, my pulse quickening. "It's not their fault. They do their best. But things can be overlooked: evidence scattered, clues lost, and the scene cleaned too soon. If someone were methodical, observant, if you thought like a criminal and took note of his patterns, more clues would emerge. You *can* get him, Inspector, but you have to be relentless, and you have to think about every angle, every stitch of story you can weave together."

He lifts his gaze, and I catch the spark in his eyes, the tension of fascination. "You think like an inspector," he says quietly, almost a whisper, as if he's afraid the room itself will judge him for listening to a woman.

"I study crime," I admit, careful to leave out the fact that I've seen the outcome years from now. "I've read every case I can, seen how mistakes happen, how killers slip through. You have an advantage, though. You're clever, and you can imagine things as they happened. If you look for those tiny details, you'll have answers that can change everything."

He leans closer, resting an elbow on the bar, and his voice lowers. "And you want to help me?"

I hesitate, caught between intrigue, panic, and desire. I can. I want to, but I don't know how much to say, or if I should even *think* of mentioning things that haven't happened yet.

"I can try."

He chuckles softly, the sound warm and kind, his eyes never leaving mine. "Even so, you've already given me more ideas than I could have imagined. You have an eye for detail."

I feel myself blush. "It's kind of an obsession."

"A dangerous obsession, perhaps," he replies, just loud enough for me to hear. There's a teasing lilt, but I can feel the underlying seriousness.

We sit like that for a long moment, the clink of glasses, the quiet murmur of a few patrons fading around us. He's handsome and confident, and I wish we'd met under any other circumstances.

Still, I can't stop thinking about Annie and all the other victims, and all the ways I *might* help Harrow catch the man who's already claimed a life.

Is that why I'm here? To catch Jack the Ripper?

# TWENTY-NINE HANBURY STREET

## *MARK*

My tea has gone cold on my desk. I can't stop thinking about Lena Carter, even though I haven't seen her in a full week. The way she analyzes a crime scene is unlike anyone I've ever met, and I keep replaying our conversation, trying to make sense of it and figure out how she knows so much.

At first, I was suspicious. A young woman showing up out of nowhere, asking questions about Polly Nichols that cut closer to the truth than anyone else dared. I wondered if she was helping the killer, if she had some hidden agenda. But the more she spoke about fingerprints, the angle of the attack, how to interpret the scene, how even minor details could reveal the assailant... the more I realized I could trust her. Not blindly, perhaps, but enough that her insight has haunted me ever since.

I don't understand how she knows so much. Boot prints, calculating the weight of the assailant from the injuries, blood splatter indicating the direction the assailant is attacked from, it all sounds impossible when most officers are still relying on witness statements and rumors. Alas, every word she said makes perfect sense. I replay it in my mind over and over, imagining how I might apply her advice tonight, tomorrow, in the next alley, and the next crime scene.

Lena is so interesting and mysterious. She's also distractingly beautiful. There's an intensity to her, a depth I can't quite reach, and it pulls at me in ways I continually try to ignore. I find myself picturing her smile, the tilt of her head as she explains something complex that I only partially understand but that I know is important. I shake my head, sip the cold tea, and try to focus on the morning reports, but her voice keeps interrupting my thoughts.

The station door creaks, and I look up, expecting a constable with some minor complaint. Instead, it's Corporal Finch, his face drawn tight, his eyes grim. "Inspector Harrow," he says, his voice low, "there's been another murder in the same manner as Polly Nichols."

My stomach lurches. "Where?" I demand, my voice sharper than I intend.

"Hanbury Street. She was found early this morning by John Davis, one of her roommates. Evidence suggests the same assailant. Nothing was taken, and she was wounded in a similar fashion."

A shudder shoots down my spine. I'd already been considering speaking to Lena again soon, but now, a sense of urgency overwhelms me. Mentally, I go over every bit of advice she mentioned about careful observation, prints, noting clues at the scene....

"Finch, gather a team. We move at once."

I grab my satchel, which now contains a stub of chalk, a pad of paper, a soft paintbrush, a few empty bags for evidence, and a length of twine. I obtained these items the day after speaking with Lena at The Blind Beggar, in case something happened, and I needed to retrieve evidence.

When Finch and I arrive, the yard is cordoned off by constables standing back, horror etched into their faces. The body is still where she was found. She's a young woman, her round face framed by sandy-brown curls, her eyes closed and skin pale, her throat slit in a clean, terrible line. She lies on the damp, grimy ground of the backyard where the people who live in the house dump their chamber pots, where refuse and muck have collected in every corner. The boot prints in the mud and blood streak across the yard like the dark footprints of the devil himself. Not only did he murder this poor woman in cold blood, he left her here like she were nothing more than garbage.

I address the men immediately. "No one step any closer. Every print counts, every smear, every bloody droplet. Nothing is to be touched."

I motion to the photographer, who's hauling a tripod and the glass plates he uses for exposures. These plates are the large, fragile sheets that capture everything in sharp detail when the shutter opens, long exposure and all.

"Take close-ups of each bloody boot print," I tell him. "Then, capture wider photos showing the prints' path and her position."

He raises an eyebrow in surprise and then nods before carefully setting up his equipment. He slides a glass plate into the camera and adjusts for light, the shutter clacking as he captures the scene.

Once the photos are taken, I move to the railing along the alley and the door handle on the house. I figure these are places the killer likely touched. I rub the chalk lightly into the soft brush, then sweep the dust across the railing, showing Finch and the greener constables how to press a sheet of paper over the surface, smoothing with care then lifting it straight up. The first faint whorl appears: a fingerprint.

They stare, their mouths slightly open as if witnessing a magic trick. "By God," one mutters, but I keep my eyes on the surface, lifting a second print from the door latch. I mark both papers with a quick sketch showing location and orientation. Every print is precious, a silent witness.

I step back and outline the body with chalk, marking the edges of her form on the ground, careful not to disturb any clues. The shape of her face, the curls matted with blood, the slit across her throat–it's all horrifying but necessary to record. I sketch the layout in my pad, noting the angle of the body, the proximity of the railing, the doorway, the line of prints. Even in death, she tells a story.

Finch measures stride lengths along the bloodstained dirt as I demonstrate. "Notice the spacing," I say. "He was moving fast here, slowing there. Weight shifts, heel to toe. All clues. They mean something." The constables copy my notes, their eyes filled with curiosity as they record.

I signal to Finch. "Go around front and find out the names of every soul living in this house."

He nods and disappears around the corner, returning a few minutes later. "Inspector, it's the Richardson house, Twenty-Nine Hanbury Street. I spoke to John Richardson and his mother, and wrote down the names of other tenants living here. The victim was killed in her own backyard, sir, Miss Annie Chapman."

Just then, Chief Inspector Frederick Abberline steps into the yard, his eyes scanning the scene with the cool, measured assessment of a man who has seen too much and refuses to be shaken.

"Inspector Harrow," he says, "report."

I summarize the evidence, the witness statements others were gathering as I collected data, the sketches, and the photographs. He nods once, brief but clear. "Satisfactory. Nothing missed. Well done."

Abberline crouches slightly, his eyes moving over the body and the alley, then he straightens. "The killer is bold. If this escalates, we'll have a serious problem on our hands. Remember, every detail counts."

With a tip of his hat, he moves on, leaving the real work to us. This behavior is right in line with what I'd expect from him or any other man in charge—arrive late, announce the obvious, and leave early.

I take one last walk around the perimeter and notice something dark lying under the nearby water tap. I step closer, kneel, and pick up a worn, leather apron. It's still damp, faintly scented with soap, and clearly has been freshly washed.

I turn to Finch. "Find out who this belongs to," I say.

A short while later, Finch returns. "The apron is John Richardson's. His mother insists she washed it two days ago, before the murder." He shrugs, handing me the apron.

I take it carefully and place it in a separate bag, noting every crease, and every scent. Two days ago, and it's still damp? Was it really just dirt? Or is someone trying to cover up blood? Something about the timing and the wetness sets off every alarm in me. This isn't a coincidence, and I can't dismiss it.

By the time we finish, the yard is lined with boards protecting the boot prints. The chalk outlines mark her position. The lifted fingerprints and glass plate photographs are packed carefully. This time, we have something more than murder and gossip. We have her story in prints, images, and careful measurements, and a trail we might finally follow to the man who did this.

When I return to the office, it's quiet except for the scratching of my pen as I make notes, trying to piece together the story of the young woman found on Hanbury Street. The more I stare at my notes, the more protective I feel of her–and all the women in this part of London. Could I have prevented this? If only I had caught the killer that night when I was chasing him near the Thames....

There's no question in my mind. This is the cruel work of the same man.

When the door opens, I look up to see Lena Carter standing there, and beside her, the redheaded girl from The Ten Bells. Both of them look concerned, tense, and wary.

"Inspector Harrow," Lena begins. "We were hoping you had a moment to speak with us."

"Yes," I reply, gesturing for them to step inside. "Please, come in. Close the door behind you."

The redhead looks petrified and is tugging at the hem of her apron, twisting it between nervous fingers. Lena's eyes meet mine. "We came to see if something happened to one of our friends last night." Lena's tone is timid.

I frown, sensing the fear in her words. "Explain, won't you?" I say carefully.

"We tried to find her," the other woman says. "We wanted to warn her, to keep her in the tavern with us, but she went out anyway, and this morning the alley behind Hanbury Street was roped off. Did they —" She hesitates, glancing at Lena.

Lena cuts in. "Was that because they found her body there?"

A chill runs down my spine. How do they know? How could they have pieced together any of this without being at the scene? I keep my tone calm. "We found a woman's body there early this morning."

The women glance at each other, and then Lena nods. "Please, can we see her?"

I grab two whistles from the table, putting them in my pocket, and then gesture toward the door. "Follow me," I say. "I want you both to see what happens when women go out alone at night. I don't want either of you hurt, and if seeing this will keep one of you from walking these filthy streets, then you need to look."

The walk to the coroner's office is short, and my mind is racing, but I try to keep my expression neutral. I can't let them see the questions gnawing at me.

At the coroner's office, we step inside. The woman's body lies on a cold slab, covered by a sheet. I pull it back.

Lena leans closer, scanning every detail. She exhales slowly. "Yes, that's Annie," she says quietly. The redhead gasps, pressing her hand to her mouth.

Perhaps it's a bit harsh, but now these women have a crystal clear picture of exactly what danger lies out there in the streets of Whitechapel.

I cover their friend back up, and reach into my coat pocket, taking out two whistles the Yard keeps for orderlies and night-watchmen. "Keep these," I tell them. "If you're ever in trouble, blow short, hard blasts. Make a noise that won't be ignored. Keep a weapon, a blade, on you at all times. Stay together. That's all I can ask."

As they leave, I close the door, leaning against it. Annie Chapman... another name added to a growing list of questions, boot prints, fingerprints, chalk outlines, and photographs. Somewhere out there, the man who did this walks free, but for the first time, I have evidence I can follow.

# SAUCY JACK

## *LENA*

SHANNON'S HAND is tight in mine as we walk back down the narrow street. Her grip squeezes painfully, like she's afraid if she lets go even for a moment, she might lose me, too. I can barely breathe through the lump in my throat.

"I still don't understand, Lena. How could you possibly have known?" Shannon's voice breaks between sobs. "How could you know Annie wouldn't make it home last night?"

I swallow hard, blinking rapidly to keep my tears at bay. "I saw the man she was with, and I just notice patterns," I say, my voice trembling. "I notice the way people move and how they react to situations. He was very suspicious. It's instinct, but it's also something I've studied. I know how to spot danger before it strikes." I squeeze her hand gently. "All of us need to be careful, Shannon, every woman on these streets. There's a killer out there."

Her head drops onto my shoulder, and I wrap my arm around her, letting her cry. Every step we take back toward The Ten Bells feels heavier than the last.

I can't get the image of Annie's face–her light brown curls, and that huge gash across her throat–out of my mind. The stillness of her body is burned into my memory.

"Lena," Shannon whispers, her voice muffled against my shoulder. "Why her? Why Annie? She was a mother...."

I shake my head slowly. "I don't know. I wish I did. All I know is that we have to be careful and watch out for each other."

When we reach the tavern, Flossie and Louisa are behind the bar, stacking mugs and pouring drinks. Their smiles fade when they see us, and immediately they know something is wrong.

"It's Annie," I whisper, barely able to meet their eyes. The words feel like heavy stones in my mouth.

Flossie freezes, a rag slipping from her hand. Louisa's eyes widen, disbelief flashing across her features. "Annie? Is she dead?" Flossie's voice trembles.

I nod, tears falling freely now, and I hastily brush at my cheeks.

Shannon pulls me close again, sobs shaking her body. "Two women," she says between gasps. "Two in a week. How can anyone walk these streets and stay safe?"

I glance at Flossie and Louisa. Their faces are as pale as ghosts, and the reality settles over all of us. The streets of Whitechapel are no longer just dirty and difficult. They are deadly, and now, more than ever, we have to be cautious, vigilant, preparing for a predator who moves unseen, striking with terrifying precision.

I let my head rest for a moment against Shannon's, feeling the heat of her tears. "We'll be careful," I promise, though the truth is that even being careful might not be enough. The killer is out there, and for Polly and Annie, it's already too late.

Shannon and I step behind the bar. The tavern is already beginning to get busy. The warmth from so many bodies and the noise hit me all at once, and the smell of spilled ale and the occasional sharp shout make anxiety creep through my every cell. I try to keep moving, but my heart is filled with regret, dread, and guilt.

I fidget with the whistle around my neck, the one Inspector Harrow gave me, and think about Annie. I'd seen her in here two nights ago and took her to a quiet corner table. "I can't tell you how I know this," I'd told her. "But if you don't stop going out at night, this will be the last week of your life. There is a man murdering women in Whitechapel, and I can't tell you how, but I know you're next."

She was intoxicated and thought I was joking at first. Then, she seemed startled by what I had to say, and I hoped she'd actually listened.

I know Annie had a hard life. She had a young disabled child in an institution, lost a teenage daughter to meningitis, and had another daughter she couldn't care for because of her drinking. Her husband left her, and the alcohol dependency that followed only made life harder. Annie's life was a grim case study in human behavior and consequence. It's something I'd usually analyze professionally, but seeing it here, in person, tears me apart. I prayed, in vain, that somehow my warning would alter her trajectory and keep her safe, but obviously, it did not.

The door swings open, and a group of men shoves inside. One slaps a hand on the counter, grinning widely, scanning the room as though sizing up the women. Flossie steps forward, her cheeks pink, speaking softly to a man who leans toward her. Louisa follows, adjusting her corset, scanning the crowd.

"There aren't any free rooms upstairs tonight. All of them are taken," Louisa mutters. "If we're gonna make any money, we'll need to take to the streets."

Flossie bites her lip, nodding. "Yes, we don't have much choice unless we take the men to our own beds, but I'd rather not have the sweaty ol' things up there."

"I'd rather let you use my bed than have you out on the street," I say. "You must not go out there. Promise me."

"We know how to protect ourselves, Lena," Louisa says, lifting the hem of her skirt to reveal a daggerette tucked into her stocking.

Flossie leans over the bar. "Yes, we carry weapons, and we stay out of the shadows. We don't walk down alleys alone."

"You don't understand," I nearly shout. "This man is not hiding or lurking in the shadows. He's going to blend in and seem like a normal customer. He's going to smile at you and charm you, and that's when he strikes."

Flossie and Louisa seem to mull over the idea, but even after my explanation, after Polly and Annie, I can tell they still don't fully grasp the danger they're in. The way they've always lived, the need to earn their money, the habits ingrained from years on these streets, still hold more sway than fear or caution. Their lack of self-esteem, the way they measure their worth by the work they do, makes tonight feel inevitable. The more they drink tonight, the lower their inhibitions become, and I fear for their lives. While neither of them are on the original kill list, it's possible my presence here has changed the timeline enough that one of them is now in danger.

A man leans over to order ale. Shannon pours, nodding politely, and I watch the women move toward him, trading soft words and brief laughs. I see Louisa's hand brush his shoulder, hear her flirtatious laugh, and my heart feels heavy.

I glance at Flossie, her eyes moving toward a different patron, a taller man with a hat pulled low. Every instinct in me screams that he could be the killer. My hands shake slightly as I set down a tray of mugs, wishing I could make these women understand fully without scaring them to death or giving up my secret.

Then, I see Louisa stagger out the bar door with a man gripping her arm, whispering close enough that she laughs and swats at his hand when it slides over her breast.

I shout to Shannon that I'll be back and follow Louisa quickly, keeping to the edges of the street. She sways as they move past darkened stoops, clearly tipsy and unsteady. They reach the doorway of a small lodging house with a vacancy sign in the window, and Louisa disappears inside with him. I linger for a moment in the street, tension twisting in my stomach, my mind racing with thoughts of what to do next.

My focus slips for the briefest instant, and then a shadow falls across my path. A hand clamps over my mouth before I can even react. I struggle, kicking and swinging my elbows. Another hand twists my arm behind my back. I bite down on his gloved finger, tasting leather, and then I scream.

He drops the hand that was covering my mouth, and I spin to face him. His face is hidden beneath a heavy handkerchief, a hat pulled low over his brow. I can see nothing but dark eyes. I kick him, hard and fast, my boot connecting squarely with his crotch. He doubles over with a sharp grunt, and my other arm slips free from his grasp.

I blow my whistle in loud, short blasts. "Get away from me!" I shriek as I run away.

The man, who has to be the Ripper, chases after me, grabbing me by my hair and throwing me to the ground. Then a sharp, commanding voice cuts through the darkness. "Let her go!"

I catch sight of him and gasp. Inspector Harrow. He runs toward us, and the attacker hesitates, then bolts, disappearing into the shadows.

Scrambling to sit up, I turn to watch him disappear into the shadows. Harrow's hand lands lightly on my shoulder. "Are you all right?" He cans the street for any sign of the man.

I nod, barely able to speak. My head hurts from him pulling my hair, but I manage to get to my feet with Harrow's help.

"I can't let him get away," Harrow says. "If I don't catch him now, he'll strike again. I'm sorry to leave you here, but I have to follow him."

I don't even hesitate. I take off running, keeping pace beside him as we sprint down the twisting streets. Ahead, the shadowed figure of the man moves quickly, disappearing between buildings. I push harder, my lungs burning, knowing we have to end this tonight.

We turn corners, leap over crates, nearly collide with other late-night wanderers, and I barely notice. Adrenaline drives me. The man's movements are frantic now, desperate, but he never looks back. Harrow shouts something beside me, a warning, but I only hear it as white noise. All I can see is him, the *real* Jack the Ripper.

The chase leads us toward the river, the street opening to the misted wharf. The shadows of the pier and moored boats swallow the Ripper, and then he's gone, vanishing into the darkness of the Thames. Harrow skids to a halt beside me, his hands on his knees, catching his breath. I stop, gripping a post to steady myself, staring at the empty space where the man disappeared.

"We lost him," I whisper, my voice weakened by the terror that's draining me. "It looked like he jumped into the river."

Harrow nods, finally allowing himself a long exhale. "Yes. This isn't the first time, either. I'm just glad you're safe. Come with me. We need to speak in private."

I glance up at him, still catching my breath, then nod. We walk back in silence, slower now, still tense. I'm expecting us to go to the station, but instead, we arrive at a modest home, and I step inside, shivering, not just from cold but from the lingering horror of a near death experience at the hands of one of the most famous serial killers of all time.

Harrow closes the door behind us and gestures toward the couch. I sink into it gratefully, still shaking, and he perches on the edge of a chair opposite me. He pours two glasses of whiskey and hands me one. "Drink," he says quietly, and I obey, letting the burn settle in my chest, soothing some of the tension.

"Tell me everything you remember," he says, leaning forward, his elbows on his knees, his eyes intent. "Every detail."

I take a deep breath and try to steady my racing thoughts. "His face… I didn't see much of it," I begin. "It was covered with a kerchief, with a hat low over his forehead. I only saw his eyes. Dark. Sharp. Evil."

Harrow listens, sipping his drink, but he doesn't interrupt.

"His hands were gloved. I bit his finger when he grabbed me, and then I screamed and blew my whistle.

He nods, his jaw tight. "Good. That saved you. I just happened to be passing by two streets over."

I nod, taking a sip of whiskey. "It seemed as though he vanished into the river. He just disappeared."

Harrow's expression tightens. "Yes. He's clever, slippery. He's done that to me twice now. I should have caught him the first time, but that was the night I pulled you from the water."

I shake my head, guilt hitting me in the gut. "I hindered you from catching him? I'm so sorry…."

He moves to sit beside me, resting a hand lightly on mine. "Listen to me," he says firmly. "You saved yourself tonight. That's what matters. We'll catch him."

I realize, suddenly, that despite the horror of the night, the fear, the chaos, this is the first time I've felt safe and protected in this century.

"They'll be calling him Saucy Jack by morning." The words tumble from my lips before I can stop them.

"Saucy Jack? Certainly an interesting moniker. How do you know that?"

"I don't know, but it suits him," I try to backpedal. "I just want to help you catch him more than anything," I whisper.

Harrow nods, his eyes meeting mine. "And we will. But for now, you must rest. You've definitely earned it." He gestures toward the bedroom. "You can have my bed. I'll take the couch."

I glance at him, stunned. "I… I can't possibly take your bed."

"You need to sleep," he interrupts gently. "You've been through enough for one night."

I allow myself to be guided toward the room, my heart fluttering at his kindness and the protection in his voice. He tells me goodnight, and I slip off my boots and crawl under the covers.

The danger isn't gone. The killer still prowls. But with Harrow near, I feel ready to face whatever comes next–and ready to help catch Jack the Ripper.

Yet, somewhere deep down, I ache for my mom, and wish I could hear her voice. I wish I could feel her comforting presence, even just for a moment. The thought of her worrying about me, and not knowing where I am, makes tonight feel all the more tragic.

Somehow, I manage to fall asleep, still feeling those deadly fingers on my skin.

# DEAR BOSS

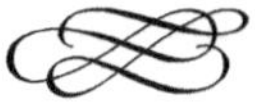

## *MARK*

THE SMELL of blood hits before I see the body. It's just after 1:00 in the morning when I step into Dutfield's Yard, just off Berner Street. The area is narrow, hemmed in by the Working Men's Educational Club on one side and a row of stables on the other. Louis Diemschutz still stands beside his cart, his face as white as my chalk, his horse stamping nervously in the muck.

"She was right there when I turned in," he stammers, pointing. "The horse shied. I thought it was just a spilled flour sack... until I touched her."

I crouch beside the body. The woman lies on her left side, one arm tucked behind her back, the other draped across her stomach. Her hand still clutches a few small cough drops wrapped in tissue paper. A scarf is knotted tight around her neck, the bow pulled to one side as if it had been yanked from behind. Blood drips from a deep wound just below her jaw, pooling black in the dirt.

"She's still warm," I mutter, brushing my fingers near her wrist. "He was here only moments ago."

Corporal Finch hovers, uneasy. "Her body is warm, though her hands are cold, and her fixed eyes are focused on the wall."

"Did any of the club members see anything?" I ask.

Finch shakes his head. "No, sir. A few left between half-past twelve. None of them noticed a thing."

I straighten, scanning the alley. The killer must've slipped out just before Diemschutz arrived. He was interrupted and forced to flee. That's why he didn't mutilate her womb like the other two victims. "Call for every copper in the area to keep an eye out. He's probably nearby."

Before I can issue any further orders, a young constable runs up, his breath ragged. "Inspector Harrow!"

I turn sharply. "What is it?"

"Another one, sir," he gasps. "Only this time, far worse. Mitre Square. It just came in."

Two women in one night? He was interrupted with this victim, so he took it out on another woman with even worse consequences. "When?"

"Not ten minutes ago, sir."

I step back from the body, enraged. "Get this area cordoned off. No one leaves. I want statements from every man who's been down this way in the last hour."

"Yes, sir."

The constable hurries off, but I don't move right away. I look down at the woman again, her pale face half-shadowed in the dark. She didn't scream. No one heard her. He cut her throat clean and quiet, just like he's done before.

I turn toward Finch. "Let's go to Mitre Square," I say. "Now."

By the time we reach Mitre Square, it's 2:00 A.M., and some of the Metropolitan Police are already here. Police Constable Watkins meets me near the warehouse gate, his face ashen beneath the brim of his helmet.

"I passed through not fifteen minutes before," he says, his voice shaking. "Quarter past one, maybe half past. There was no one here then, nothing and no one."

I follow him through the iron gate and stop cold. She's on her back, her head resting against a coal hole, turned toward her left shoulder. Her eyes stare blankly, her mouth open, the bonnet fallen behind her head. Her throat is cut clean through, deeper than the one on Berner Street. Across her neck is a blood-dark kerchief. Her arms lie by her sides, palms up, her fingers curled, and her dress is drawn up above her waist.

I force myself to take in every detail, every wound. Her right leg is bent the left extended straight. Her intestines are drawn out, smeared with filth, draped deliberately over her shoulder. A section of her intestines has been severed entirely and placed under her arm. This was her punishment for being second after his first victim's mutilation was disrupted.

The stench of blood and human waste hits my throat. I pull my notebook from my coat pocket and begin to write, forcing my hand to stay steady. *Face is mutilated beyond recognition. Lobe of right ear severed. No signs of bruising on the body. No spurting of blood on bricks or pavement. Death quick. Throat cut first.*

Watkins paces a few steps away, wringing his hands. "I swear to you, sir, I saw nothing. No sound, no movement. I just—"

I cut him off. "You did your job. He works in silence. He's done this before."

I study the jagged, savage cuts, the way her body has been torn apart with deliberate cruelty. Whoever did this knew exactly where to strike, and her womb is ripped away. "This isn't just murder," I murmur, anger knotting my stomach. "He hates women. He's punishing them with every slash."

"He's a butcher," Corporal Finch mutters.

"Her right earlobe is severed. Neatly took it clean off," I say, looking up at Finch. "Anything interesting about that to you?"

"Yes, sir. The letter, sir."

"Precisely."

We search the square, but there's nothing this time. There are no bloody footprints, no discarded weapon, not even a drag mark. Chief Inspector Abberline arrives then, his presence steadying the less experienced constables. Some of the green lads are pale and gagging at the sight, barely able to keep their stomachs down. Together, we methodically comb the area again, checking every corner and shadow, but still, the square offers no trace of him.

I glance at my pocket watch. *2:12 A.M.* She's still warm. That means he was here less than thirty minutes ago.

By dawn, every inspector in Whitechapel will know what I've seen tonight. Two victims in the same hour. The Ripper's temper is escalating.

It's nearly 3:00 when I'm summoned to Goulston Street. A police constable, Alfred Long, waits by the stairwell of a tenement, his lantern casting a sickly light on a doorway.

"There," he says, pointing. "When I came by at twenty past two, it wasn't here. Swear to it."

At the base of the stairs lies a torn scrap of white cloth, soaked with blood and streaked with something fouler. I kneel, examining it… a piece of apron. "From the woman in the square?"

"Has to be. Covered in blood and dung."

I note the location, sketching it in my book. Just above, chalk scrawled on the black brick wall reads: *The Juwes are the men that will not be blamed for nothing.* The letters are crude and uneven.

A murmur rises among the gathered officers. Antisemitic whispers spread fast in Whitechapel; this could ignite a riot by morning.

"Get Warren here," I order.

When Commissioner Charles Warren arrives, he stares at the wall in silence, his jaw clenched. "If this stays up until daylight," he says, "there'll be blood in the streets. Wipe it off."

"But sir," I protest. "It is evidence—"

"Wash it. Now."

After we photograph the graffiti, and I search for fingerprints, a constable scrubs the words from the bricks. I copy them into my notebook before they vanish forever, though it feels like erasing a clue carved in bone. Still, Warren is the top brass, the head of the Metropolitan, and I've no say in the matter. When the commissioner gives an order, even if it's tearing a clue from the wall, we obey.

The piece of apron is taken for evidence. I bag it myself. It reeks of rot and excrement. The Ripper must've carried it with him after

Mitre Square, wiping his hands before he vanished again into the labyrinth of alleys.

As I walk away, the city begins to stir. Somewhere, a cart rattles over stone. Life continues, indifferent, but all I can see is what's left of her face. He wasn't interrupted the second time. He took his time.

I close my notebook, the ink smearing under my thumb. "You're still out there," I whisper to the dark. "And I swear to God, I'll find you."

Three days ago, I sat in my office and read the letter the killer sent the newspaper from start to finish until the letters blurred. I remember the red ink smudged where the writer had scrawled "Jack the Ripper" as if he meant it to be a jest. I copied it word for word in my notebook and circled every phrase: "funny little games," the talk of clipping ears, the ginger-beer bottle full of "proper red stuff."

Lena had called him "Saucy Jack" days before the letter appeared. I have no explanation for it, and the thought needles me all the same. I trust her, but sometimes the things she says, the way she seems to *know* what's coming–it's damned strange.

I try to make the clues fit into a face, a trade, a route. I mimic the handwriting, the slope of the letters, the way the Hs hook. I tell myself the letter was a hoax because journalists like a headline, and the public likes to be frightened. Still, I keep thinking about the ear, that small, obscene detail. If it was a boast, then someone knew how to wound with intent. If it were a prophecy, then clearly, we are already too late.

Now, there are two women dead in one night, the second butchered in a way that reads like a lesson. The letter tucked in my pocket is a promise. I've gone over it until the edges are soft, and the ink has set into the grain of the paper, every "ha, ha" an insult, every boast an attempt to shape us, the police, into the audience he wants. I hated the smugness in it then. I hate it now with a white hot, personal fury. It's not only the mutilation that eats at me. It's the contempt. He imagines himself above us, a conductor pulling strings while we fumblingly follow the music.

Anger makes me precise. The ledger, the docket of names, the paper with the letter folded inside–I sharpen each fact against the next, forcing a pattern where there's chaos.

I walk the lanes with my coat collar up and my hands in my pockets because thought needs motion. I find Lena at The Ten Bells, serving drinks as usual.

When I sit at the bar, she pours me a glass of whiskey. "Rough night?"

I toss it back in one gulp and don't beat around the bush. "Want to come to my place? I need to speak to you."

She studies me for a long breath and then nods once. "All right."

She tells the redhead she works with that she's leaving, and we step out into what's left of the night together. We walk shoulder to shoulder, and Lena's presence beside me comforts the ache in my chest.

Inside, I set the letter on the table between us.

"Is that the Dear Boss letter?" Lena asks softly.

"Yes. For three days, I've been reading it and trying not to let it teach me how to hate." My voice is rough. I force a breath. "Tonight, it's taught me that he can do worse. He's not just killing. He's showing us the rules of his game. I want to end it."

I strike a match, light an extra lamp, and the yellow glow swells into the room. Lena shrugs off her shawl and sits at the small table already scattered with notes, sketches of alleyways, witness statements, and the letter. We've done this before, more times than either of us will admit to anyone else. Two, sometimes three nights a week, she'll come here after her night's work at the tavern and my rounds at the Yard, and we'll stay up until dawn fitting fragments together: scraps of evidence, human behavior, the shape of a man I've never seen but we both can feel.

This early morning, the work feels heavier. I unroll the map of Whitechapel across the table and weigh the corners down with glass mugs. "Here," I say, marking Berner Street. "And here—Mitre Square. Less than a mile apart, maybe forty-five minutes between the deaths. He's walking. Not running. He's very comfortable in the dark."

She taps a finger on the margin of the "Dear Boss" letter. "What about this line—about the ear? It could be a coincidence, or he could've meant it."

"What do you mean?" I ask, hoping she's having the same thought as me.

"If I were going to fake a letter to a newspaper just to grab headlines about killing women, promising to cut off an ear would be the perfect flourish: sensational, grotesque, and plausibly linked to a throat wound, so the papers would eat it up."

"Precisely, and yet tonight, one of the women's ears was nearly cut off."

"So it's probably not a coincidence. That letter was likely really written by the killer. We may never know for certain. It's too bad the papers didn't know to fingerprint the letter before everyone in London touched it." She sighs.

"My thoughts exactly. Now, he's just taunting us. Two in one night wasn't merely impulse. It was testing limits, seeing how much time he could take before we closed in."

We go on like this for hours, piecing together distances, handwriting loops, the color of the ink, even the type of paper–cheap, mass-printed, sold by the thousands of sheets near Fleet Street. At some point she yawns, resting her head in her hands. When I look again, her eyes are closed, her breathing slow. The clock reads nearly 6:00.

"Go on, then," I murmur, standing. "Sleep."

I take her arm gently, just enough to guide her to my bed in the next room. She sits on the edge, and I remove her boots. When she lies down, I pull the blanket over her shoulders and step back. Even asleep, she's beautiful with her soft pink lips and long blonde hair falling in loose curls around her face. I can't help but stare for a second, watching how peaceful she looks. I shut the door halfway. The couch is rough, the springs uneven, but it's worth it to have her here where I know she's safe.

The next morning when I awake, the world feels just as brittle, and Lena is gone. I shave, knot my tie, and walk to the Yard through a tin tinged sky. When I reach my office, the constable at the door straightens and says, "There was a letter for you slipped under the door. It's on your desk, sir. No one saw who left it."

I take the envelope. Same cheap paper, same slanted hand. The margins are smudged with something that might be blood. My stomach sinks before I even break it open.

**Dear Inspector,**

*I see you've found yourself a clever little helper.*

*Is your bird as sharp as her teeth? She bit me and kicked me, you know? I wasn't even going to hurt her. I just wanted to see if she wanted to go home with me. Ha. Ha.*

*Best keep her close before I do.*

*Good luck.*

*Yours Truly,*

**Jack the Ripper**

The few lines on the page harden my anger into something cold and methodical. This is no longer just my profession. Now, I have a single, fierce purpose: to keep Lena safe. I don't care about headlines or procedure right now.

I will hunt the Ripper until there is nowhere left for him to hide.

# JUST A LITTLE CRUSH

## *LENA*

THE TAVERN SMELLS like gin and sweat, the same as it has every night since I started working here. Shannon hums as she pours drinks, her fiery red curls shining in the lantern light. I scrub a sticky spot on the counter, though what I really want is to close my eyes and wake up in my bed in 2025. Coffee instead of gin. Electricity instead of gaslight. My mother's comforting voice instead of this constant, crawling fear.

Four women are gone, four faces that won't stop haunting me no matter how many times I tell myself there was nothing I could've done. Polly, Annie, Liz, Catherine—names carved into my mind like scars. I replay every moment I might've changed something. If I'd arrived a week earlier. If I'd remembered the exact dates of the killings. If I could've found the Ripper before he found them. I studied these murders endlessly, read every account, watched every documentary I could find just trying to understand the killer, but I didn't memorize the details. God, I wish I would have.

Then, there's Mary Jane Kelly. She's the one I can't stop thinking about, the one I might still save, if only I can remember her death date. November, I think, early November, but the memory slips away every time I reach for it.

I glance at Shannon. She's got that brightness to her, that careless kind of life people cling to in this part of Whitechapel. Her disarmingly kind personality draws people in. "You all right, love?" she asks, catching me staring.

"Oh, I'm fine," I say too quickly. Then, before I can stop myself, I add, "I just wish you and the girls wouldn't go out at night anymore."

She arches a brow. "We know. You've told us every day for weeks." She winks.

"I mean it," I say. "After what happened to Annie…."

Shannon freezes for a moment. The noise of the tavern swells around us, the fiddle player, the drone of conversation, the occasional shout from the poker game, but the tension between Shannon and me tightens.

"I saw," she says finally. Her voice is quieter now, stripped of the teasing edge she usually carries. "Don't think I'll ever forget it."

"Then please stay inside. Work here or upstairs tonight. Just, please, don't go walking the streets at night. Please."

She shakes her head, setting the rag aside. "It's better money out there. Men pay more for company when you find them, unlike the ones who've been spending their money on booze and losing at poker all night here." She smiles, but I see the sadness in her eyes. "And I grew up here, Lena. I know these streets better than anyone. I can take care of myself."

"No one can take care of themselves out there," I whisper.

She steps over and squeezes my hand. "You're sweet to worry, but this is Whitechapel. Worry doesn't change a thing."

I wish I could tell her that I've seen what's coming, but I can't without sounding crazy. Shannon and the other girls already think I'm insane for hanging out with a cop almost every night of the week. Telling them I'm from the future would definitely make me look truly nuts. So I just nod, and the guilt burns like cheap whiskey in my throat.

Louisa and Flossie drift in, laughter following them as they shrug off their shawls. "We'll take over for a bit," Louisa says, already ducking behind the bar. "Shannon's due her turn, ain't she?"

My stomach knots. "She doesn't have to go out tonight."

Flossie rolls her eyes and takes the rag from Shannon's hand. "'Course she does. It's Friday. The docks'll be crawling with sailors and easy coin."

Shannon flashes me a grin that's meant to reassure me, but it doesn't reach her eyes. "Don't fuss, love. I'll be fine."

I step closer, lowering my voice so only she can hear. "Take your whistle. Promise me."

She pats the small tin whistle she wears around her throat. "I always do."

"And stay where the lamps are bright. Don't go down the narrow alleys. Don't cut through anyone's yard, even if you know them. He waits in places like that. And Shannon, don't you ever, *ever* follow anyone who leads you toward the river. Stay away from the Thames."

She laughs softly. "Yes, mum."

"I mean it." I hope she can hear the desperation in my voice. "If you hear anything, if anyone follows you, blow that whistle and run as fast as you can. Go somewhere well lit, and don't stop until someone comes."

"I will." She gives me a hug. "You've got a good heart, Lena." She pulls her shawl tight around her shoulders and slips out the back door into the cold, damp night. The door clicks shut, and the sound of it echoes like finality.

I stand frozen, staring after her until Flossie nudges me with a smirk. "You might be taking this Ripper business a bit too serious, eh?"

My gaze snaps to her. "You have *no idea* how seriously you should be taking it." I haven't told them he actually attacked me. I couldn't find the words.

Louisa stops pouring ale and glances between us. "You talk like you know something we don't."

I don't answer. I can't. Instead, I lean on the counter, trying to steady my breathing, trying not to picture Shannon disappearing into the shadows of Whitechapel.

Louisa clears her throat, changing the subject. "That brooch of yours, you wear it every night. Certainly is a pretty thing."

My hand goes automatically to the small pin fastened at my collar. "I found it by the river," I say quickly, "a long time ago."

"It looks just like one Polly Nichols used to wear," Louisa says, tilting her head. "Strange, that."

The words hit me like a punch to the gut, but I manage a small, tight smile. "Must be a common style."

"Perhaps so." Louisa shrugs and goes back to serving drinks, but my heart won't slow down.

Polly. The first victim. I close my fingers around the brooch. I wonder if the brooch really did belong to her and if it helped me travel back in time.

The tavern door opens, and a gust of cold air sweeps through. Every sound in the room dulls as Inspector Harrow steps inside.

He looks exhausted tonight, with dark shadows under his eyes, but still he's unfairly handsome. He's the kind of man who would be considered handsome in any time with his dark wavy hair, strong jawline, and the confidence of a man with nothing to prove to anyone other than himself.

"Evening, Miss Carter," he says, his voice low and rough as he steps up to the bar. My heart flutters, and warmth rushes through me, just like it does every time he's near. "I was wondering if you might like to join me for a late dinner?"

I glance at Louisa and Flossie, who are pretending to polish mugs but clearly watching. Then Louisa leans on the counter, smirking. "No one believes you two are just friends anymore, you know." She winks, and I glance at Mark, who seems to have just the slightest blush on his cheeks.

Flossie grins, adding, "Don't worry. We'll hold the fort here, and we won't wait up."

I shake my head, laughing, then turn back to Mark. "I'd love a late dinner."

He nods, his eyes bright. "Good. Shall we?"

We walk arm in arm through the narrow streets, the lack of electric signs and street lights causing it to be much harder to see than when I walked these streets with my cousins, Ella and Tom. It's no wonder the killers of this era got away without a trace. And yet, I don't mind the dark when Mark is beside me. He's the only one in this city that makes me feel safe, and strangely at home, even though I'm centuries out of place.

Mark's house always smells faintly of tobacco and ink, the familiar scent of him that always seems to settle my nerves. He lights the lamps, shrugs off his coat, and glances at me over his shoulder.

"I'm afraid it's nothing fancy tonight," he says, pulling a small pan from the shelf. "Eggs and toast will have to do."

"That sounds perfect," I answer, and it does. The simplest things with him always feel perfect.

He cooks while I sit at the table, watching him move, focused, his sleeves rolled up to the elbow. When he slides a plate in front of me, the eggs steaming and the toast browned just right, something about the small domestic act makes my throat tighten. He's so kind and considerate, which is a rare treasure in this grim city.

We eat quietly for a few moments before he breaks the silence. "I've been back through the Chapman scene again," he says. "Compared the fingerprints with John Richardson's. They match, but they would, wouldn't they? He lives there. Any trace of him means nothing, and when the Ripper tried to hurt you, he was wearing gloves. We could be picking up prints from people who were simply passing by."

I nod, keeping my tone calm. "What did you find when you compared the fingerprints from each of the scenes?"

"We found the same thumbprint at three of the scenes, but when we measured them against the men we picked up, there were no matches. And the boot prints are just as frustrating. Some of the suspects fit, but it's a common style. Half the East End's wearing the same bloody boots."

He sets his fork down, the frustration in his voice unmistakable. "Eddowes was different," he says, quieter now. "The face. The brutality. It's as though he hated her for being a woman."

The anger in his voice trembles beneath the surface. I reach out and touch his arm. "He hates women, and he hates prostitution. If we could figure out why, it would lead us closer to the truth."

"Most men in Whitechapel claim to hate prostitutes until it's three in the morning, and they're a pint deep."

"Yes. We're looking for a specific type of man, though, one who has deep internal issues with women. Someone whose mother was cruel to him, or someone whose wife left him for another man. When we find the killer, it'll be no coincidence that he's lived a tragic life and has some deep-seated feelings of contempt for a specific woman or two who hurt him. That's why he doesn't just slit their throats but cuts them in the parts of their bodies that make them women."

"That's... remarkable," he says, his voice low and edged with disbelief. "How do you know that?"

"I've read over many cases. Many, many murder cases. There are similarities between all the murderers I've learned about."

"Lena, sometimes I think you should have my boss's job."

I wish I could tell him I've taken more classes than any of his bosses. I've seen too many documentaries, and then I'd fill him in on everything from forensic psychology to DNA, but that would mean admitting I'm from one hundred and thirty-seven years in the future. No matter how close we've become, that's a risk I'm not willing to take.

After the dishes are cleared, we move to the small couch near the fire. I sit beside him, closer than usual because it feels natural, but there's a difference tonight. I can feel it. We are becoming more comfortable with one another, and in that comfort, we're discovering romance blooming in the midst of our friendship.

I lean my head against his shoulder, and almost instantly, he lifts his finger under my chin, and tilts my face toward his. I look up, and then his lips are on mine.

The kiss is urgent, and full of longing. I move my hands to his chest, and he wraps his arms around my waist, holding me close.

We kiss deeper, hungrier, and I can't remember the last time I felt this alive, this safe, and this *seen*. Every brush of his lips, every press of his hands makes something inside me unravel and reassemble at the same time.

Eventually, we break for air, but I don't back away. I rest my forehead against his shoulder, still pressed to him, still tasting him, and still holding onto him. He sinks back into the couch with me still wrapped around him and lets out a long breath. A few minutes pass, and then I notice the soft, even sound of him snoring.

I bite back a laugh, careful not to disturb him. He's so tired from working and worrying about the case. Finally, I whisper his name. "Mark."

He stirs and murmurs something. Gently, I slip up from the couch and guide him to his bed. The moment his head hits the pillow, he's asleep again.

I curl up on the couch, pulling my shawl tight around me like a blanket. My mind spins, not with fear or danger tonight, but with thoughts of him, the sexy cop who is only one hundred and sixty-five years my senior. It's so ridiculously funny when I think of it that way, and yet, I am smitten. The way his lips feel on mine, the way I feel when he looks at me, and the way he's saved my life more than once has me wondering if this might be more than just a little crush. I still don't know why I was sent to this century, why I'm trapped in this time. But I'm certain of one thing: meeting him was worth everything.

I close my eyes and feel my body relax, and a small, contented smile creeps onto my lips. I'm falling for him, fast and sure, and for the first time since arriving in 1888, I let myself feel at home.

# PERFECT COVER

## *MARK*

I WAKE to the scent of tea drifting through the house, warm and comforting. When I step into the kitchen, morning light cuts through the curtains, falling on Lena crouched over a stack of my notes. Her pen scratches against paper with a precision that makes me pause. She's reviewing my sketches from the crime scenes, the witness statements, and the few observations I've managed to gather about the Ripper's movements.

I've never met a woman so focused and clever. I look at her with admiration. She doesn't flinch at the violence or the grime. She doesn't look overwhelmed by the unfamiliar. She absorbs it, dissects it, and makes sense of it with a clarity I can't help but envy.

"Good morning," she says without glancing up. "I've started breakfast. Did you get some sleep?"

"I did, thank you." I sit at the table, watching her move around the small kitchen, her shawl draped over her shoulders as she sets a pot on the stove and turns back to the table, flipping through my notes again. This morning, her hair is pinned up like a golden halo. She's so fair, I feel that familiar tug in my chest. Even the danger of the world outside fades a little in this moment with her.

"Tea?" she asks, setting a cup in front of me and gesturing toward the small plate of ham and eggs she's prepared.

"Thank you," I murmur, taking the cup. The warmth seeps into my hands. I try not to stare, but I can't help it. There's an elegant rhythm to her movements, and it feels good… I feel better when she's here. I can't remember the last time mornings felt this quiet, contained, and almost normal. It's nearly enough to make me forget the streets outside and the monster we're chasing.

After we eat, I set my fork down, glancing at Lena. "I was thinking. If you want, you could come with me today. I'm going to visit a few of the addresses tied to the murders."

She smiles enthusiastically. "Really? You mean you want me to come along?"

I nod. "Yes. I could use another pair of eyes, someone who notices details I might miss."

Her excitement is almost tangible as she gathers her notebook and pens. "I'd love to go with you."

"Good. Then let's get started. We have a lot to cover today."

She stands a little straighter, energized, and for a moment I can't help but think how alive she makes even the ghostly streets seem.

We start at the street where Annie Chapman was killed. I knock on the door, and an older woman opens it.

"Good morning," I say. "We were just checking back in to see if you've noticed anyone lurking at night since the event that took place in your backyard. Seen anyone cutting through the back alley since that night?"

She shakes her head, hesitating. "I don't see much. It's too dark back there at night, and I go to bed early most evenings anyhow."

"Has anything been out of place?" I press gently.

"What do you mean, Inspector?"

"Have you noticed anything in your backyard that has been touched or moved since the crime scene was closed? Or perhaps anything out of place or missing from your home?"

"No, sir, not that I've noticed."

I thank her for her time, and we turn to leave.

We move on to the Working Men's Club. A man is stepping out as we arrive.

I step forward and offer my hand. "Good morning. Inspector Mark Harrow. Were you here on the night of the murder?"

The man nods. "Yes, I was here that night until eleven."

"Did you see anyone unusual? Perhaps a man with a kerchief over his face and a hat pulled low on his brow?"

"No. No one who looked like that, but I did see the lady who got killed. She was tipsy as a loon, wandering around asking to bum a smoke, asking if anyone wanted a date."

"Did anyone take her up on her offer?"

"Not that I saw. Someone lit her a smoke, and then we all went back inside. She hollered something about how she'd be here if we changed our minds."

I ask about any strange noises, arguments, or anyone loitering longer than usual. He tells us he didn't hear anything, and we move along.

The third stop is near where Catherine Eddowes was killed. We speak to a constable who was on patrol that night.

"I passed through about fifteen minutes before the murder," he says. "Everything was quiet. Nothing unusual."

We note it, then move on. When he leaves, Lena nudges me.

"Mark, I think he's lying."

I laugh. "A cop? Why would he lie? And why do you think he's lying?"

"His shoulders were tense when he said the patrol was normal. He kept flexing his hands and avoiding eye contact when you asked about the timing. Maybe he wasn't doing his rounds thoroughly, maybe he's covering up the Ripper's tracks... or maybe he's the murderer," she finishes.

I laugh, at first lightly, shaking my head. "Come on. A cop?"

But the more I think about it, the more it chills me. A police officer knows the streets, the patrol routes, the schedules. They'd know when every street is empty and when no witnesses are around. Perfect access. Perfect cover.

"Damn," I mutter. "You're right. A cop would have been able to move unnoticed and know exactly when to strike...."

She nods. "And if he felt he could get away with it, he would. Watch for inconsistencies in patrol reports. That's where you'll find the truth."

I'm quiet for a moment, my eyes meeting hers. "Lena," I say finally. "You truly see people."

She shrugs lightly. "It's just connecting the dots. Most people talk too much or too little. If you're paying attention, you will notice everything in between."

I feel a sense of clarity I haven't felt since the Ripper started his murders. We haven't caught him yet, but with Lena at my side, the pieces are beginning to line up. The more I watch and listen to her, I realize that it's not just her intelligence I admire, but her intuition, her calm authority, and the way she sees through the chaos without panic. I trust her instincts completely, and for the first time since the killings began, I feel like we might finally have a chance to catch the bastard before he strikes again.

By evening, as we walk back to my house, I find myself unusually quiet. The streets bustle around us, but my attention is elsewhere. Lena moves beside me, her notebook tucked under her arm. I watch her—the way she tilts her head when she's thinking, the faint crease in her brow when she considers a clue—she is so incredibly beautiful.

I can't stop thinking about last night and the way her lips felt against mine. I shouldn't admit it, but I keep replaying it in my head—the heat of her hands, the softness of her touch. I liked it even more than I thought possible.

I hadn't allowed myself to admit it before, but it's undeniable now: I'm falling for her. She's brave, clever, and resourceful in ways I've never encountered. Every time she notices something I miss, every time she sees the truth in people before I do, I feel proud to know her. I can't bear the thought of her walking these streets alone, facing danger.

We reach the door to my house, and I hold it open for her. She thanks me with that small, almost shy smile, and for a second, I let myself imagine a life where she isn't constantly at risk, one where she stays close enough that I can breathe easier.

I can't stand the thought of anything happening to her. It frightens me how much I care for her. All I want is to keep her safe and close enough that I can make sure no one harms her. I want her here, with me, and the force of that need is stronger than I can ignore.

I could ask Lena to stay, to claim it's to keep her safe, and of course, that wouldn't be a lie. But what I really want is for her to feel she belongs here with me.

# FALLING FOR HIM

## *LENA*

INSIDE MARK'S LIVING ROOM, a fire flickers against the soot-dark walls, throwing gold light across the coffee table where our papers are spread like a map of obsession. We pore over patrol schedules, witness statements, lists of constables and their assigned routes. Some part of me clicks into the same methodical focus I used in case simulations back home, back when I was studying to be a forensic consultant for the NYPD, analyzing patterns of violence. Now I'm doing it here, a century and a half too soon.

Mark pours whiskey into two glasses and hands me one. He sits next to me, his sleeves unbuttoned, rolled up, and his collar loosened. He always looks so ruggedly handsome.

"Three constables were near Hanbury Street the night Chapman was killed," he says, tapping the edge of a report. "Only one of them claimed to check the alley near where her body was found, but look at this. His timing doesn't line up."

I lean in, tracing the lines of his notes. "You mean Parker?"

He nods. "He said he passed through at 5:45 A.M. That's also around the time a witness saw Miss Chapman speaking with a man in a low hat and long coat. If he had taken his regular patrol route at the normal time, he would've seen Miss Chapman, too."

I take a sip of whiskey, feeling its warmth rush through me. "But he swears he saw nothing."

"Precisely. So did he not see the murderer because he's working with and protecting him?"

"Maybe he just didn't do his rounds at the right time—or did he commit the murder?"

I shuffle through another stack of papers. "What about the constable from Mitre Square, the one who found Eddowes?"

"Watkins. He's solid. Reported every round precisely, but the patrol after him, Clarke, has a discrepancy there, too. Twenty minutes are unaccounted for."

"Two constables, both with missing time." I glance up at him again. "You think they could've been working together?"

He shakes his head slowly. "Perhaps. Or maybe one of them just stopped to smoke. I could be seeing ghosts where there aren't any."

"Or maybe the ghosts are real," I say. "Some killers can't stop themselves from replaying the same ritual, no matter the risk, and the Ripper fits every psychological hallmark I've ever studied."

Mark smiles. "You have a brilliant mind, Lena. I can't keep up with you sometimes."

"Why, thank you. You're pretty smart yourself, Inspector."

He looks at me then, and electricity sparks between us. It's been building for days now, in the way his hand sometimes brushes mine when he passes a pen, in the way his voice softens when he says my name, but tonight it's clearer. His gaze lingers, unguarded, and I feel it everywhere at once.

I clear my throat and turn back to the table. "You're staring, Inspector."

He grins, unashamed. "Am I?"

"Yes," I say, but my voice is different, breathless. "You are."

He doesn't look away. "I can't help it."

Our usual banter is gone, replaced by affection, something intense, and yet, disarming.

He leans back, studying me. "You always surprise me," he says. "You see things before I do. You make sense of what I can't."

"That's because you're too close to it," I tell him. "You've been chasing him for too long to see straight."

The fire crackles, scattering light across his face. I look at him, and the realization hits so suddenly it almost hurts.

I'm falling in love with him.

It's ridiculous. Impossible. I'm supposed to be in my own time, where this case is history, and he's just a name buried in old newspapers. But here, now, he's flesh and blood–warm, alive, and looking at me like he wants to taste more than my lips this time.

I sip my whiskey, trying to quiet the ache in my chest. "Do you ever wonder," I ask softly, "why things happen the way they do? Why people meet when they shouldn't have had the chance?"

"I do. I think about it all the time now."

The words settle between us like a confession neither of us meant to speak. We should be thinking about the killer and the victims. I should be thinking about getting back home to my mom, but all I can think about is Mark. I want to help him find the Ripper. I want to end this nightmare with him. But more than that, I don't want to leave his side.

Mark pours the last of the whiskey into our glasses and lifts his toward me. "To catching the bastard," he says.

I raise mine. "To catching him."

Our glasses clank, a sound that feels to me like a vow. We both drink, and then Mark leans closer, his hand brushing mine. It's a light touch that sends a current through me.

"Lena," he says quietly, his voice roughened by whiskey and lust. "Tell me this isn't just me."

I look into his eyes. "I feel it, too."

He exhales, a sound halfway between relief and surrender. His hand slides to my cheek; I forget how to breathe, and then he kisses me.

It starts softly, cautiously, but the second I lean in, it deepens. I can taste the whiskey on his lips. When we finally part, my heartbeat is wild in my chest.

Mark rises, pulling me with him, the papers scattering across the table as we move. He tugs me toward him and kisses me again, more passionately this time, with a kind of need that matches my own.

When we part, he twirls me around until my back is pressed against his chest. His lips find my neck, and a whisper of ecstasy rushes up and down my spine. I press myself against him and place his hands on my breasts. He squeezes them through the thin fabric, and my nipples harden under his palms. A moan escapes my lips as he starts guiding me toward the bedroom.

Once inside, the door clicks shut behind us, and he pauses, looking at me with desire. Our fingers brush against buttons and laces as we undress each other, peeling away layers of clothing with shy laughter and heated glances, until nothing separates us.

We tumble onto Mark's bed together, our bodies pressed close. His hand rests lightly behind my head, his fingers tangling in my hair as he leans down to kiss me again.

This time, his hands slide over my bare breasts, teasing me into bliss. Every time he touches me, I become more and more ready for him.

When I reach for his hardness, he groans and kisses me deeper. I slide my hand up and down, and his eyes lock on mine, a rough, hungry growl escaping him.

His lips find my breasts, and my moans become even louder. My body instinctively melts into his touch, every tension unraveling.

"I can't wait to feel you inside of me, Inspector Harrow," I whisper.

"You have to be the most desirable woman I've ever met, Miss Carter." He looks up at me, desire darkening his gorgeous eyes, and positions himself between my thighs.

Mark slides up and down my folds, igniting a fire I can't contain. I grab his biceps, urging him closer, pressing into him.

When he finally fills me completely, the sensation overwhelms me, and I cry out, my body convulsing with pleasure. Our bodies move together in rhythm. Every stroke drives me higher, my body desperate for more. I shiver and shudder again as wave after wave of bliss crashes over me, and then I feel him follow, our movements locking us together in a bond that's fiercely intimate.

We finish, and he lies on his back next to me. I wrap my body around him, my cheek resting against his chest. He kisses the top of my head, his fingers tracing the arm I have curled around him. There's a softness in the way he holds me. I feel protected in his arms.

Tonight, everything else fades as we fall for each other.

# RED INK

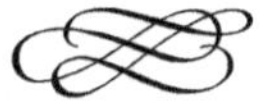

## *MARK*

WHEN I LEAVE MY HOUSE, Lena's still at the table, her bare feet tucked beneath her, reading through one of the witness statements I brought home last night. She's wearing one of my shirts, though it hangs loosely on her. When I reach for my coat, she looks up, stunning and radiant, every inch of her beautiful to me.

"Do you really have to go?" she asks, almost pouting in an endearing way.

I hesitate, caught between duty and the pull of staying and looking out for her. She stands, coming closer, and presses a hand to my chest.

"Goodbye, Mark," she whispers, and her lips touch mine.

When she pulls back, I ask, "Will you be here when I get back?"

"Yes, of course." She smiles brightly.

"Good," I murmur, brushing my thumb over her cheek. "Lock the door. Answer it for no one."

Her eyes narrow, shadows of worry clouding there, but she nods, pressing another kiss to my cheek. I inhale her scent, memorizing it, and then drag myself away, forcing my feet to move.

Last night was amazing. It wasn't impulsive or sudden but the inevitable beginning of something we'd both been trying to resist. Weeks of working side by side, arguing and agreeing over evidence, and sharing coffee until dawn–somewhere between all that, we'd stopped being friends and became something more. Last night, it all caught up with us, and it was incredible.

I can still feel her against me as I walk, the ghost of her touch like heat under my collar, and now, as I travel to work, I can't seem to think of anything or anyone else.

I keep my head down, trying to focus on the day ahead, but my mind drifts to her laughter and the way she'd fallen asleep with her head on my chest. After everything this city's shown me, it still feels strange that someone so good could even exist here.

When I reach the station, that fragile peace cracks. The constables' voices carry into the hallway.

"Says he can catch a killer by his fingerprints now."

"Waste of bloody time, if you ask me."

"Going soft, that one."

I keep walking. Let them talk. It doesn't matter what they think. It only matters that I catch the bastard, because if I'm wrong, another woman dies.

My desk waits near the window, papers stacked high, but when I approach, I see there's something new lying in the center. It's an envelope like the first two, with my name written in red.

"Where'd this come from?" I ask.

Finch glances up from his notes. "Found it this morning, sir. He must've slipped it under the door last night.

The sight of the handwriting makes my stomach turn.

*Dear Boss,*

*So you've taken to chalk and prints now, eh? Clever tricks won't save you. I see your pretty little helper, the fair one with the long blonde curls. You ought to keep her close. Wouldn't she make a lovely letter of her own? Red ink and all.*

*Yours truly,*

*Jack the Ripper*

*P.S. I'll carve you a lesson soon enough.*

Immediately, I put on gloves and start dusting the letter for prints, every motion precise and controlled, though I am enraged.

I imagine Lena's face. Every flirtatious glance, every laugh, the way it feels when she holds my hand, and I feel the pull to protect her. This letter is a threat, and I'll treat it as one methodically, yet with fury burning under the surface. I dust the edges, the corners, looking for anything that can lead me to him. I'm furious, focused, and I won't let him touch her ever again.

Standing, I walk the length of the office, pretending to study the noticeboard. The constables keep their distance, wary of me. Men who gossip are always the first to step back when real danger shows its teeth.

I pick out the ones I'm watching: Parker by the ledger, leaning in the corner, and Clarke near the lockers, shoving a pipe back into his pocket. Every man here knows I've been taking prints, but only someone inside could have known enough to write this letter. That thought narrows my focus. If the writer is one of them, it could very well be Parker or Clarke. They're ordinary enough to be safe from suspicion, and that's what unsettles me.

I tell Finch I need the duty rosters from the last month. "For cross-checking," I say, keeping my voice flat.

He gives me a strange look but fetches the papers without comment. I spread them across my desk, my pencil tapping the wood as I jot down dates and names. Parker signed off a dozen late shifts, and Clarke switched with a colleague twice in October. Neither has a proper alibi for two nights in particular, and what's more, they're nights that women died.

Handwriting is a habit as much as a sin. I pick up a slate of notebooks, routine deposit slips, and constables' logbooks. My eyes, trained on letters and loops for years, begin to pick at small things: the way a lower-case G curls back, the peculiar hook on a Y, the way the writer of the Ripper letters dots and I with a hard, impatient stab instead of a gentle mark. Parker's ledger has neat, disciplined counters; but there's one page where his hand drifts, the Y in "yellow" has that same jag as the Y in "yours."

I'm fully aware of how dangerous it is to put all my coins on a loop of ink, and yet, I also know how dangerous it is to ignore a pattern.

Could one of them been the killer? Donned a black hat, a scarf over their face, and a long coat? It's possible–isn't it?

I catch Constable Briggs in the hallway. He's a quiet sort who has only been here a year. "Briggs, come with me. We need to speak where we won't be overheard." He follows without question, and I lead him into an empty office down the corridor, closing the door behind us.

I keep my tone casual, letting the question slip in like rain. "You work the night shift with Parker and Clarke, don't you? Seen anything unusual from either of them lately?"

Briggs shifts slightly, his eyes moving to the floor. "Parker sometimes disappears for a walk, sir. He says it clears his head. Clarke... keeps to himself mostly."

I file it away. Sometimes the smallest, most ordinary details are the ones that matter most.

I won't confront either man yet. I tuck copies of the rosters and the matching samples into an envelope and lock it in my top drawer, under the false bottom where I keep my private reports. I'll need more: dates, witnesses, a reason these officers were or weren't where they claimed to be.

My plan will start with observations and end with proof. When I'm certain enough to act, I'll take them in front of the others and show them the truth. Until then, I'll remain calm.

The evening walk home seems to take longer than usual. I keep thinking of Lena, the sunlight in her hair, and the thought of her waiting for me pulls me along harder than the exhaustion ever could.

When my house comes into view, the windows glow soft against the dark sky, and for a moment, I feel at peace. I step inside to the smell of garlic, onions, and something hot sizzling in the pan. Lena turns at the sound of the door, wooden spoon in hand.

"You're home!" she says excitedly.

"I *needed* to get back to you," I answer, and it's the truth.

She turns and steps forward, wrapping her arms around me. I drop my coat on the chair and hug her back, feeling the weight of the day fall away for just a moment. Her lips press against mine in a gentle kiss, and for a second, I feel comfortable relief.

She pulls back and rests her head against my chest. "I missed you," she whispers.

I kiss the top of her head and hold her for a second longer before she goes back to making dinner. The knife on the board, the hiss of the fire, a gorgeous woman cooking for me–it all feels too good to be true.

Dinner is simple, but it tastes better than anything I've had in weeks. She talks about the witness statement she'd been reading this morning, about a theory she has concerning the alleyway behind Hanbury Street. I listen, half-distracted, until she notices.

"What happened?" she asks. "Something's wrong."

I pull the letter from my coat pocket and lay it on the table between us.

"It came this morning," I say. "He slipped it under the station door. I took prints from it while half the station house gawked."

She unfolds it carefully. Her eyes move across the page, and all the color drains from her face. The air changes then. The fire hisses, the clock ticks louder, and it all feels like a trick of time.

"He's watching," she whispers. "He's obsessed with us."

I nod once. "And that's why I'm keeping an eye on Parker and Clarke. I don't yet know if they're involved, but I'll be watching every move they make."

She reaches for my hand and tightens her fingers around mine. "We need to find a way to lift their prints and compare," she says. "I so wish there were DNA testing."

"DNA testing?" I ask, confused. "I confess, I've never heard the term."

"Uh... it's new," she stammers. "More sophisticated than finger-prints, though I fear we lack the proper tools to employ it here."

"Some new American notion, is it?"

"Yes," she says quickly.

"That's tragic," I whisper "To think the answer might exist and *still* be out of reach."

She offers a weak smile, but I can see the worry behind her eyes.

I turn toward the letter again. "No matter. I'll find another way. Parker and Clarke… I know at least one of them's hiding something. I'll get their fingerprints and compare them to these."

"I'm really beginning to think it could be one of them."

"I am too, and I aim to prove it before this bastard has another chance to come near you."

"Just be careful," she says.

"I will," I tell her. "And I'll be bloody well damned if I let the Ripper anywhere near you again."

# TOO MANY PENNY DREADFULS

## *LENA*

I WAKE up in Mark's arms, and for a second, I let myself feel safe. The world outside is still, the streets quiet, and for the first time in days, I don't feel that cold dread pressing against me. But it's early morning, and the day is young. He wakes, too, stretches, and we get dressed, moving through the morning together.

"I'm going out today," I tell him.

His gaze moves to my face instantly, worry weaving through his expression. "Where to?"

"The Ten Bells," I say. "I haven't seen Shannon in a couple of days, and she's probably worrying about me. I'm worried about her, too."

He steps closer, placing his hands on my shoulders. "Be careful," he murmurs, leaning down to press a kiss to my forehead.

"I will," I reply, offering a reassuring smile. "I'll be back before dark. I promise."

He holds me for a moment longer, then finally lets me go. "All right, but stay sharp and alert. You'll need a knife, your whistle, and a key to my house."

I feel a thrill at the word *key*. I've never had the key to a man's house before. It's small, but it feels significant, intimate, and it's a symbol that I'm welcome here, that I belong in this part of his life.

He hands me the knife first and then the key on a small ring.

"Thank you for being so considerate of me," I whisper, and I mean it.

Mark kisses me, and when he pulls back, he lifts my shawl off the hook and slides it onto my shoulders, straightening it and fastening it for me. I giggle at the attention, and he winks, a teasing glint in his eyes.

"Stay safe," he says before turning and leaving for work.

The walk to The Ten Bells is long, but the sun is bright, and I don't feel as threatened as I would if it were dark. Still, there's a wariness that never fully leaves me, not while the Ripper is still out there.

When I push open the door, the bell jingles above my head, and I'm immediately greeted by familiar voices.

"Lena!" Shannon's face lights up, Louisa's too, and Flossie claps her hands in delight.

I laugh, relief washing through me, and hug them in turn. I'm so glad they're all three together, safe and well.

"You must tell me everything about your love affair with the handsome inspector. Don't skip a detail!" Shannon takes my hand and guides me up the narrow staircase to her bedroom.

Once inside, I sit on the bed I borrowed that first night and so many nights after. It feels like a lifetime since I was home in 2025.

"I'll probably be staying with Mark for a while," I start gently. "Don't worry about me, but please, Shannon, you must keep yourself and the other girls safe. None of you should go out at night. The Ripper is still out there."

Shannon frowns. "They still have no idea who he is?"

"No, and now he's taunting Harrow with letters. He's going to kill again. I know it for a fact, and Shannon, you're too good, too kind, too young and beautiful to… just promise me you'll stay inside at night, no matter what."

Shannon swallows hard and nods firmly. "I promise."

"You're one of the best friends I've ever had," I say. "I love you."

Shannon's sapphire blue eyes brim with tears, and she gives an anxious half-smile. "I love you too, Lena. Are you quite certain you're all right? The inspector… he treats you properly?"

I laugh, nodding. "Yes, he's extraordinary. He's so wonderful, thoughtful, and handsome, of course. I'm really happy there with him."

Her lips twitch into a wry smile, a faint flush tinging her cheeks. "That's very good to hear. I'm glad, truly. Well, I must get back to work, but I'm positively relieved you came back to show us you're in one piece. We were fretting something terrible about you."

"I'm fine, really," I reply, grinning. "You don't need to worry about me, but do take care of yourselves, all the same. There's a killer loose in these streets." I hug her once more. "Goodbye, Shannon."

She squeezes me back. "It's not really goodbye, then. I'll see you later, you saucy wench."

I follow her down the stairs, my heart a touch lighter after our conversation. The chatter and clatter of the pub grows louder, and I wave goodbye to Flossie and Louisa as I step onto the street.

The sunlight is now a warm, golden glow. I make my way back to Mark's house, each step a reminder that I'm still here and that I've survived another day in this strange city and this even stranger time. Yet, the truth overwhelms me with every stride: survival isn't enough, not when I know what's coming. Not when I know *who* he'll kill next.

Mary Jane Kelly.

Her name echoes in my mind. I've met her only once, briefly, but I can't forget her–tall and striking, with bright red hair like Shannon's and a pretty face. She's so full of life, and she's out there somewhere in these streets. If I don't act soon, she won't be for long.

*I'm going to have to tell him.*

The thought makes my stomach roll over. Mark isn't like anyone else here. He listens. He sees me. And somehow, he makes me feel safe. I trust him with my life, and yet, what I need to tell him is insane.

*By the way, I'm from the future, and I know who Jack the Ripper kills next.*

He'll think I'm completely looney tunes.

Still, what choice do I have? I slipped up already, rambling about

DNA like it was common knowledge, watching him stare at me in confusion while I tried to backpedal. I can't keep lying if I want him to trust me and if I want to save Mary Jane.

By the time I reach his house, the sun has started to dip behind the rooftops, the light dimming. I fish the key from my pocket. The lock clicks softly, and I step inside.

The familiar scent of tobacco and ink greets me. I relock the door, hang my shawl on the hook, and head to the kitchen, rolling up my sleeves. If I'm going to tell him something that could ruin everything, I might as well do it over dinner.

I find potatoes in the cupboard and eggs in a basket, and set to work. I imagine, just for a second, what it would be like to have a life here with him.

I hear a key jingle, and the front door opens.

"Lena?" His deep voice carries down the hallway.

I turn to the sound of is voice, wiping my hands on a towel. "Hello, handsome."

He appears in the doorway, his coat still on, his hair windblown. "It smells good in here," he says.

"Fried eggs and potatoes. It's not much."

"It's great. I'm starving."

He steps closer, and I rise on my tiptoes to kiss him. It starts soft, tentative, then becomes even more passionate. I can feel in his kiss how much he missed me today, and it makes my heart melt, but it also makes what I'm about to tell him even more difficult to say.

His hand lingers against my jaw when he pulls back. "Did you have a good day?"

I nod, my heart thudding. "I did, but there's something important I need to tell you."

He studies me, sensing the change in my tone. "Very well." He slowly pulls out a chair. "Go on, then."

Before I do anything else, I fix us each a plate and hand him his before sitting down across from him. Then, I draw in a breath. "This is going to sound incredibly strange."

Mark gives me a crooked smile. "Stranger than what you've told me already?"

"Stranger than all of it."

"I'll try to keep up."

I exhale and look down at my plate instead of his face. "I'm not from here. I'm not from this time. I'm from the future."

Silence fills the room. When I finally look up, his brow is furrowed, his mouth a thin line between disbelief and concern.

"From the *future*," he repeats, as if testing the words.

"Yes."

He studies me for a long moment, then laughs, like he thinks I'm joking. "You've been reading too many penny dreadfuls."

"I'm serious, Mark. I came from the year 2025. That's how I know so much about the crime scenes."

His smile falters. "Lena, come now—"

"I know what's going to happen next," I cut in. My voice shakes, but I can't stop now. "Next, he's going to kill Mary Jane Kelly. She's going to be murdered like the others. I can't remember the exact date, but it's soon. He'll kill her in her room in Miller's Court, and there will be so little of her left, she'll be almost unrecognizable. I saw the photos. Mark, they're more gruesome than *even you* can imagine. They say it will take him about two hours when he does this to her. I know. I've seen the very photos that your office will soon take."

He goes still, the color draining slightly from his face. "How could you possibly—"

"Because," I say, my voice cracking, "where I come from, it's history."

He shakes his head slowly, as though trying to clear it. "That's absurd. You're asking me to believe you've somehow travelled through time."

"I know how it sounds," I whisper. "But you asked me before how I knew things I shouldn't. I didn't tell you, but I knew about the Dear Boss letter before you brought it home. I know how he works because in my time, these murders are famous history. Mary Jane's murder will be next."

He stares at me, still trying to make sense of it, and I can see doubt fighting with curiosity in his expression.

I take a deep breath and continue. "There's another reason I recognize the pattern so easily. In my time, I was about to go to work with the New York City Police Department. I'm a forensic psychologist, a criminal profiler. My job is to study killers, to understand what drives them, and to predict what they'll do next."

He rubs a hand over his face. "I can't believe that until I see it with my own eyes. Why would you say such a thing? That's... good God, that's madness."

"Mark, what I'm saying is true," I say, stepping closer. "DNA isn't an American thing, Mark, it's a *future* thing."

He blinks, caught off guard. "DNA? You mentioned that last night. What in blazes is it?"

"It's what makes us who we are. Every person, every living thing, has it inside them. It's how we'll one day catch men like Jack. We will catch them with their own blood, their spit, their hair, their very cells. DNA tells the truth even when they lie."

Mark's eyes narrow, the skepticism in them edging with the curiosity that always seems to burn just beneath the surface. "So, you're saying that one day, someone could take a drop of blood, or a hair, and know exactly who committed a crime?"

I nod, keeping my voice calm. "Exactly. They'll be able to tell who someone is just from the smallest trace of them. Skin cells, blood, saliva, anything left behind at a crime scene–it'll all speak the truth."

He exhales slowly, pushing his chair back with a screech. Then, he starts pacing the length of the kitchen. "And you've seen this happen?"

"In my time, it's how we catch criminals. We don't have to rely on guesswork, rumors, or luck. DNA evidence is irrefutable."

I can see the gears turning behind his eyes. Finally, he leans his hands on the table, studying me with an intensity that makes my heart race. "And you know who the next victim is because you're from the future?"

"Yes," I whisper, reaching out to touch his arm. "That night you fished me out of the river, that's when I came back in time. That's why my clothes were so strange. I know it sounds impossible, but that's why we can stop him. We can't wait for him to strike again. We have to stop him first. Many people in the future think he gets on The Tube after he commits these crimes, especially after Mary Jane Kelly. That's why we have to follow her. We have to protect her."

"The Tube?"

"Uh, the underground railroad. We call it The Tube in the future."

For a moment, I think he might still dismiss me as mad, but then his tone softens. "All right, Lena. I'm trying my best to believe you. We do this carefully. No one can see us. No one can know."

I nod, relief flooding me. "We'll follow her and keep her safe without her ever realizing it. If we can protect her, maybe we can stop the rest of his murders, too. I just wish that I could remember the exact date of her death so we wouldn't have to follow her all the time and risk making her uneasy."

"Yes, that would help, but I'm sure it'll be soon. He did just write that letter. He will strike again. We'll begin tonight," Mark says. "We watch, we wait, and we make sure she gets home safely, every night until we discover who the murderer is."

We eat our dinner quickly, and then I gather a small satchel with essentials. The streets darken as night falls. Every alley and passage feels like it could hide the Ripper. A cold dread coils in my stomach. I can't bear the thought of being separated from Mark for even a second. If I lose him, I could be the one the killer finds.

And no one at home even knows where I am. I long to be back with them, with my mom, my family, and friends. I long to return to the life I was meant to lead. But here I am, trapped in this time, and I know I have to make it back safely, not just for me, but for them, too.

# WHO IS HE?

*LENA*

IT'S one of those rare quiet Saturday mornings. The fog has finally lifted from the street outside, and pale light spills through the kitchen window, making the steam from our tea look silver. Mark sits across from me, eating toast, his notebook lying open beside his plate.

We got up early and have been talking for hours—two people from different centuries, trying to make sense of the same mystery.

"So," I say, stirring my tea, "in my time, one of your suspects, Aaron Kosminski, is still considered a possibility, even after more than a hundred years."

Mark looks up, intrigued. "He's still a suspect in your time?"

"Yes," I confirm. "They tested Catherine Eddowes's shawl for DNA, and it matched his DNA profile. Does that mean he's the Ripper? Not necessarily, but he was definitely in contact with her the night she was killed. From what I've studied, his behavior fits the classic profile of a serial offender. He's socially isolated, with deep resentment toward women. They typically target victims in a pattern that escalates over time."

Mark leans forward and jots down a note. "Perhaps we need to focus on him. I'd even like to have Finch trail him each night."

I nod. "That wouldn't be a bad idea. Didn't you have a witness put him at the scene of the crime shortly before it happened?"

Mark flips through his notes. "Yes. Right here." He taps a line with his finger. "There was a witness, Israel Schwartz. He said he saw Kosminski there that night, but the statement was later withdrawn."

"Probably because he was threatened," I say quickly. "Kosminski could've seen him and threatened to harm him if he didn't retract his statement."

Mark nods. "Or perhaps the poor witness was uncertain. Still, it fits, doesn't it? Kosminski is not of sound mind."

"Yes, that was in the case file as well. In a couple of years, he'll be institutionalized for threatening his sister with a knife."

"If that doesn't say Jack the Ripper, I don't know what does."

"Exactly. I would have him followed by two constables, but that's just me," I reply.

"It's strange, isn't it?" he asks. "That even more than a century later, no one's sure who did it. The case is never resolved, and the victims can never really rest in peace."

"I'd love to see if we can change that. Speaking of things that never change, I wish Shannon would stop going out at night. She's putting herself in danger."

"Yes," he sighs, rubbing his temple. "I worry for her, too." He glances up, meeting my eyes. "Perhaps I can give you some coin, and the two of you could go shopping. Buy some new clothes for both of you, and give her some extra money to keep her off the streets until we've caught the bastard."

"That might work," I admit, if I can convince her to accept it. "Thank you so much, Mark."

"You're welcome." He smiles, obviously glad to help.

He takes one of his old coast from the hook and helps me into it, straightening the collar and hands me some money, then gives me my key, whistle, and knife, just like he always does. Once I have every-thing, he opens the door for me and presses a quick kiss to my cheek before I step out.

Mark is always so thoughtful, and I can't help but beam as I walk down the street. Being around him makes me feel protected and at home, a feeling I haven't had in a long time. Knowing I'll return to him this evening makes me want to rush, but today is about Shannon.

As I step into the bustle of Commercial Street, I feel a pang in my chest. I've been so focused on survival and the murders that I haven't allowed myself to think about my family for a while. My mother, my cousins, my friends—none of them know where I am. I wish I could reach through time and space to see them, to reassure them that I'm alive. I miss them terribly, more than I can admit, but I push the thought aside. That can't happen, and there's work to do.

I find Shannon at The Ten Bells just after noon. I hear her before I see her, her laughter rising above the clang of tankards and chatter. She's behind the bar, her red hair pinned up beautifully, a glass in one hand and a rag in the other. When she sees me, she waves. "Lena, love! Come join me."

I move behind the bar, and lean close so I don't have to shout. "How would you like to go shopping?"

Her brow arches. "Shopping?"

I nod. "Inspector Harrow gave me some money. He thought we might like a day out, to have a bit of fun."

Her grin is instant. "Well, you don't have to ask me twice. I'll ask Louisa and Flossie to cover for me."

When we step out onto Commercial Street, the shops are alive with activity. Wooden shutters are open, merchants arrange bolts of cloth and other wares, and the tang of dye and tallow hangs in the air. Shannon links her arm through mine, speaking eagerly about finding a green dress, bright and bold.

The first shop we enter has rows of dresses in rich velvets and dark silks hanging from brass hooks. Lace gloves are piled in baskets beside feathered hats, and a mannequin near the front wears a wine colored gown.

I touch the fabric of the nearest dress and sigh with awe. It's coarse and heavy by modern standards, but the craftsmanship is extraordinary. The Victorian hand-stitched seams, the tiny buttons, and the delicate embroidery at the collar are gorgeous. It feels like stepping straight into a museum exhibit, except I can actually try it on.

Shannon holds up a deep blue dress with puffed sleeves. "What d'you think? Would it make me look respectable enough?" She winks.

"Respectable and elegant," I say with a smile.

She laughs and twirls, the skirt flaring around her boots. For a while, we forget everything else. We try on hats with ridiculously long plumes, leather and lace gloves, and cloaks so long we'd probably trip if we wore them out on the street.

Shannon slips into a green dress and spins in front of the mirror, laughing as the skirt flares with each turn. "Oh, I love it! It suits me," she says, grinning.

I pick out a soft silver gown and try it on, while Shannon tries on gloves with delicate pearl buttons. For a while, there's nothing but fashion, laughter, and the two of us pretending to be someone else, just for fun.

At last, we settle on a few dresses: Shannon's green one and a couple more with colors and trims that make her eyes light up. We hand over the payment, and Shannon hugs the parcels close, her cheeks flushed. "Thank you, Lena," she says, beaming. "I can't believe you two got these for me."

"You deserve them," I tell her.

We're halfway down the street, our arms full of wrapped packages, when I notice a man loitering across the road, watching us with an intensity that makes my skin crawl. His coat is long, his face pale and hollow, his dark eyes shifting nervously when I look directly at him.

"Do you see that man?" I whisper.

Shannon glances over her shoulder and rolls her eyes. "Oh, him? Yes. He follows me everywhere lately. He comes into The Ten Bells and says he likes me."

My stomach drops. "Who is he?"

She shrugs. "Oh, what did he say his name was? He told me the other night. Aaron something. Works as a barber down the road."

My heart pounds. *Kosminski.* "Shannon," I say urgently, "we need to find somewhere safe to go. Now."

She frowns but lets me tug her into a small coffee house nearby. It smells of roasted beans and sugar, and the tables are crowded with factory clerks and shopgirls. We order tea and sit in the back corner, keeping our heads down until the man outside finally walks away.

When I'm sure no one's listening, I lean in. "That man is Aaron Kosminski. He's *very* dangerous. He's one of the main suspects in the Ripper murders."

Shannon gasps, her hand flying to her mouth. "I thought he was just a harmless, albeit strange, man who had taken a liking to me."

"No, Shannon. It's more serious than that. Please, listen to me. You need to stay at The Ten Bells, or stay in your room. *Don't* go out at night, not until Mark and I can find the killer."

She swallows hard. "You really think he's the one?"

"I think he could be," I say quietly, pressing a few coins into her palm. "Mark and I are so serious about keeping you safe that he wanted me to give you this. Buy what you need, but promise me you'll stay home and keep safe."

Her voice trembles when she answers. "All right. I promise."

The soft rose color that usually kisses her cheeks subsides, her face turning ashen, and for the first time, I believe that I've gotten through to her, and she'll keep herself out of danger.

We reach The Ten Bells just before dusk. Stepping through the pub door, the familiar scent of whiskey and pipe smoke wraps around us. Louisa is behind the bar, her sleeves rolled up, while Flossie clears glasses from a corner table. Both look up when we come in, their eyebrows lifting at the sight of all the parcels.

"I hope you brought us back a present or two," Louisa calls.

"Of course we did," I say, setting the packages down on the nearest table. I turn to Shannon, who's smiling from our afternoon. "You had fun, didn't you?"

She nods. "Other than the odd man who watches me too closely, it was the best day I've had in ages."

I glance at all three of them. "Listen, you know about what's been happening in the streets," I say, keeping my voice low. "But now there's someone following Shannon. I need all of you to stay inside until we catch the murderer. Understood?"

Louisa's smile fades first. "What do you mean, someone's following you, Shannon?"

Our friend shifts uneasily. "It's true. His name is Aaron Kosminski. He's been hanging around the pub for weeks, and sometimes when I run errands, I notice him following me."

Flossie frowns. "You think he's the one doing the killing?"

"I don't know," I admit. "But he's dangerous enough to make me worry. Until they catch whoever's behind these murders, no one should leave after dark."

Flossie swallows hard, nodding. "I know that man. He's a barber, and you're right. He is an odd one. We'll stay in tonight."

"Good." I force a small smile. "Now, before you think I came empty-handed…."

I lift two of the boxes and hand one to Louisa and one to Flossie. "These are for you. A couple of new dresses so you can still feel lovely, and you won't have to step a foot outside."

Before I leave, I pull Shannon into a hug. "Please," I whisper. "Be safe."

She nods against my shoulder. Then, I leave and head for Mark's house.

By the time I arrive, the sun has dipped below the rooftops, leaving the sky a dusty rose. When I use my key and step inside, the first thing I notice is candlelight flickering over the dining table, casting the whole room in a romantic glow.

The table is set with simple elegance. Roasted chicken, rosemary mashed potatoes, and fresh bread scent the air. I step closer and see two glasses of wine, candlelight glints off the rims.

"You did all this?" I ask as he helps me with my coat.

"We've both been working hard. I thought I'd do something to show you how much I care about you."

A warm-and-fuzzy sort of comfort settles over me, the feeling I've only ever experienced around someone who genuinely shows how much they care about me.

We sit, and for a while, life feels almost normal. We talk about anything but the case, his childhood, and then mine. I tell him a little more about the future, about things I miss and things I've seen, careful to keep it personal. I don't want to ruin the moment by talking about what I've learned about the case today.

After we finish, he clears the plates and then takes my hand. "Before we go out tonight, would you like to join me in the bedroom?"

I stand, press my lips to his, and let my kiss answer for me.

He guides me down the hall, still holding my hand, and we slip into the bedroom. He closes the door behind us, and I stay close, aware of the heat of his body, the strength in his arms, and the confident way he moves. Every masculine feature makes it impossible to look away from him.

When he undoes his shirt, his hair, usually combed back, falls forward with a boyish, impish charm. His eyes are alive, expressive, holding that mix of challenge and mischief that always makes my pulse race. The shirt slips open, revealing the muscles I know are strong enough to hold him above me while he takes his time, and just the sight of those biceps makes wild lust spread through me with delicious anticipation.

Mark pulls his shirt fully off, his muscles flexing as he does, and spins me gently so I'm facing away from him. He unlaces my corset and lets my clothes fall to the floor. He turns me back around and pauses, his eyes roaming over me before he slowly slides his pants down. We climb onto the bed, the tension between us electric.

He pulls me close and kisses my neck, his hands exploring my breasts. My nipples harden under his palms, and my breath comes faster. Instinctively, I spread my legs and reach for him.

Mark catches my hand before I reach him and shakes his head, a smile playing at his lips. "Not just yet," he murmurs, his voice low and rough. "I think I ought to take care of you first."

He lowers his head between my legs, and my body reacts instantly, a shockwave of warmth running through me. Every nerve in my body feels alive, and I can't help pressing closer to him, my fingers gripping his shoulders.

Mark's lips and tongue tease me, making me buck and grind

against him, and every touch sends ecstasy through me. Dizzying waves of pleasure roll through my body, leaving me trembling, yet he follows my every movement.

He holds me exactly where he needs me in order to keep me on the edge. I writhe under his mouth, lost in the pleasure only he can give. Heat coils through my body until it erupts in pure release, leaving me completely consumed by him.

After taking a second to catch my breath, I move so that I'm on top of him, feeling the strength in his arms as he holds me close. Every movement locks us together. I lean forward, letting my breasts brush against him. Mark groans as I slide down onto him, the sound full of want and need.

He places his hands firmly on my hips, and the rhythm we find makes me pick up speed..

His hands roam along my sides, guiding me, and I move with him, letting myself sink into the sensation of being completely wanted and completely taken care of. The moans that escape our lips fill the room.

When we finally find the sweet spot that sends both of us spiraling, it's impossible to hold back. Our bodies respond together, every nerve alive and screaming, and I cling to him as the pleasure crashes through us, leaving us both trembling and gasping, completely spent in each other's arms.

We lie still for a few moments, then Mark rolls onto his side. "You're so beautiful," he murmurs. "I wish we could stay in bed together all night, but it's getting late, and we have a job to do."

I nod. "You're right. We should go. Mary Jane will be leaving the tavern soon."

He kisses me once more, long and bittersweet. Then, we pull our clothes back on quickly, buttons fastened and laces tied. Once ready, we step into the street, moving toward the trail we need to follow.

"Mark," I murmur as we walk, keeping my voice quiet. "I have some news about Aaron Kosminski."

# GUILT AND BONE

## *MARK*

I DIDN'T BELIEVE Lena at first when she claimed to be from the future, but then I remembered something I had taken note of weeks ago. She'd called the killer "Saucy Jack" the night before the newspapers did. And when I considered all the information she told me that no one in this city could know–details about the victims, about Kosminski, evidence I hadn't shared with anyone–I knew she was telling the truth.

When Lena explained DNA, which is something I'd never heard of, and I could see she understood it like it was common sense, there was no denying her story.

There are smaller things, too, such as how her family never came for her, how she can read people and situations, how she understands criminals in ways I've never been taught. Piece by piece, everything she says and does adds up.

Tonight, we'll walk through the narrow streets, ducking into taverns and bars, looking for Mary Jane.

"I saw him today," Lena says, her voice almost a whisper as we step into a dimly lit alehouse. "Aaron Kosminski. He's been following Shannon."

I frown, keeping my eyes on the crowd. "I'll be damned. Following her where?"

"Everywhere," she says. "I saw it with my own eyes today while we were shopping. He shadows her errands, waits outside the shops, and then he goes into The Ten Bells. He sits at the bar and talks with her. She said he told her how much he likes her."

I shake my head. "I hope Shannon and her friends promised you they'd stay inside at night until we catch this monster."

She nods, her gaze sweeping the streets, and then she stiffens. My eyes follow hers, and there sits Mary Jane Kelly in a nearby tavern, sitting at a table near the window with a man. She's laughing and flirting, utterly oblivious to everything else around her.

I nod to Lena, and we slip inside and take a table nearby, close enough to keep her in sight but far enough away so as not to be suspicious. From here, we can watch her every move and make sure she's safe.

"Shannon and the other girls did promise me they'd stay put tonight," Lena says quietly. "Thanks to your idea and the money you gave them, they can afford to stay in for a few nights. I think they're taking it seriously this time since they realize Aaron is dangerous even if he's not the Ripper. I hope that by following Mary Jane, we'll finally catch Aaron, or whoever Jack the Ripper really is."

I watch Mary Jane laugh a little too loudly, her hair falling over her eyes in messy waves. She's beautiful, and I want to warn her and pull her out of here before something happens, but I bite back the words. Lena already tried to warn one of the victims, and it did absolutely no good.

I stare at the man Mary Jane is speaking with and realize it's not Kosminski. We settle in, quiet and watchful. Jack the Ripper is out there, and every laugh, every flirt, every step Mary Jane takes could bring her closer to him.

When they finish what's left in their mugs and rise to leave, I nudge Lena, and we follow at a careful distance, slipping through alleys until they reach a small, unmarked doorway. The man knocks, and a muffled voice calls something back. He shouts, "Victoria!" The door swings open, and they disappear inside.

I glance at Lena. "This is a disorderly house," I murmur.

She frowns. "A what?"

"A place where people pay for uh… company. Drinking, gambling, nude women everywhere, and much worse than any tavern you've been inside of. I don't really want to take a lady like you inside. Most of these houses are tiny, just a few cramped rooms with smoke-stained walls. Chaos and lust."

"We call those orgies where I come from," she says.

I feel a surge of amusement. "And have you ever been to an orgy, Miss Carter?"

"Of course not, but up until recently, I'd never traveled back in time, either."

I shake my head, and we step up to the door. I rap once. "Who is it?" a voice calls from the other side.

"Victoria," I say. The lock clicks, the door swings open, and we slip inside.

The room is dark, lit only by a couple of oil lamps, and it reeks of gin, sweat, and cheap cologne. Men lounge in chairs with naked women draped over them. Laughter, whispered requests, and moans float through the haze of tobacco smoke. Mary Jane perches on the man's knee, his hands on her breasts. As she leans away from him, the lamplight catches pale curves where her dress has slipped low.

I scan the room. "We need to blend in," I whisper in Lena's ear. "Stay close to me, but keep your eyes on her. If anyone's watching us, they'll see a couple too busy with each other to be watching anyone at all."

Before she can answer, I press Lena against a shadowed pillar, and her body melts into mine instantly. Our mouths collide in a heated kiss, our hands roaming. She bites my lower lip, and I groan against her mouth. My hand slides down to her bottom, pulling her tight against me. The warmth, the closeness, it's a frantic, almost guilty pleasure, but it's also the perfect camouflage.

When we break apart to check on Mary Jane, she's straddling the man's lap while two women lean close, pressing against him, all of them pleasuring each other.

I lean into Lena for another kiss, tasting her lips, and remembering how good she felt earlier. Every so often, I break away just long enough to glance at Mary Jane to make sure she's still here before returning to Lena, the two of us hiding in plain sight.

I glance at Mary Jane again, and she's tugging her dress back on, straightening it, and then brushing a stray strand of hair from her face. The man presses a few coins into her palm, and she takes them without a word and tucks them into her pocket. She buttons her dress the rest of the way, wobbling slightly, flushed, drunk and unsteady. Then, she makes her way toward the door, leaving him behind.

I grip Lena's hand. "Now," I murmur.

We follow behind her, keeping a careful distance. I'm worn down from working all day and into the night, but I force myself to keep moving, hoping she's heading home.

We follow her down narrow streets, and she sways with each step, her dress slipping slightly from one shoulder. Her arms flail as she struggles to keep her balance, and she bumps into a lamppost, loudly letting out a curse. Lena and I follow her all the way to her apartment, where she fumbles with the lock, nearly falls over, and then goes inside.

We sit on a bench across the street, close enough to see her apartment. Hours pass. Mary Jane never leaves her room, and no one else comes or goes. Lena tugs her coat tighter beside me, and I shift to get comfortable, keeping my eyes on the dark window.

"Nothing's happening tonight," I mutter. "We've been here long enough. Let's call it a night—"

"No," Lena interrupts, her voice tense. I glance at her. The look on her face is serious. "There's something about tonight. I know it was early November, and this night... I don't know, it just doesn't feel right."

I frown but don't argue. "Finch and Briggs are following Kosminski tonight," I murmur. "They're sticking together, watching him every time he goes out. If it's him, we'll know."

"That's good," Lena says. "But I have a feeling tonight might be the night we need to watch Mary Jane more closely than ever."

Minutes crawl by. I glance at the watch in my pocket. I swear I can hear my heart beating over the silence. Finally, I mutter again, "I'm going to call it. It's freezing, Lena. Nothing's happening."

She shakes her head again. "We need to stay a bit longer. Just a little."

I look down the alley at the fog thickening and sigh. "Fine, another half hour."

Movement catches my eye: a figure exiting Mary Jane's building. He's a tall man, his coat long and dark, a hat pulled low over his eyes, gloves on his hands, and a kerchief wrapped around his face. My pulse spikes.

He freezes, glances toward us, and his eyes lock on mine. For just a second, everything slows, and then he bolts.

"After him!" I yell.

We sprint across the slick street. He's quick, and I'm damned tired of chasing the bastard. When he turns a corner, we follow him into the stairwell leading down to the underground platform.

The narrow steps are steep, with iron railings on either side. We take them two at a time. At the bottom, the train waits, its doors open, ready to depart. He lunges toward the carriage just ahead of us. I reach out, my fingers snagging the edge of his coat for a split second, but it's useless. The doors slam shut, and the train jolts forward, metal grinding against metal, and then he's gone, swallowed by the darkness.

We stand panting, staring after the train as it disappears into the underground tunnel. "All I saw were his eyes," I say, still gasping for air. I glance at Lena. "Did he look familiar to you?"

She leans forward, hands on her knees, trying to catch her breath. "No, nothing but his eyes. It was definitely the same man who grabbed me, though."

Slamming my hand against a pillar, I growl. "How does he keep getting away like that?" This is the third time I've chased the bloody bastard, and it's getting damned ridiculous.

One look at Lena, and I realize what's happened–we didn't save Mary Jane.

"I... we..." Lena's voice cracks, and she buries her face in her hands. Sobs shake her shoulders. "We were right outside the whole time. We didn't hear anything. We could've stopped it from happening!"

I wrap my arms around her, trying to console her. She clings to me, quaking, and I feel her tears soaking into my coat. "Shhh," I murmur, though the words feel hollow as my throat tightens.

"He must've been inside waiting for her when she got home," she chokes out. "How stupid are we? How horrible are we? We just let it happen."

I want to argue, want to tell her it's not our fault, that we couldn't have known, but I can't. The guilt is suffocatingly heavy.

"We have to go back," I finally whisper, my voice rough. "We have to see... what happened."

Her body stiffens, and she pulls away, tears streaking her face. "I—I can't," she says, shaking her head violently. "I saw a picture once... one picture of her body. I can't. It's enough to make me sick to my stomach."

I nod, understanding but still aching. I can't let her go in, and yet, I have to see it. I take her hand and lead her to the stairwell. If she won't even look, how bad must it be? My stomach twists, bile rising, but I step toward Miller's Court anyway, Lena close beside me, still sobbing and trembling.

The door to 13 Miller's Court is ajar, and this close, I can see broken glass in the window pane nearby. That must've been how he got in. I swallow hard, trying to brace myself.

Inside, the room is small, every surface scuffed and worn. The fire has died to cold ashes, the faint smell of burned cloth lingering in the air. On the bed, the horror of it strikes me immediately.

Mary Jane Kelly lies there, mutilated beyond recognition. Her throat is cut, her body torn, parts rearranged with a deranged meticulousness. One breast is removed. Her abdomen is mutilated, the mess clearly staged. Her clothing lies folded in the corner, except for what is smoldering in the fireplace. The room is silent but for the distant drip of water somewhere behind the walls, each echo making the scene feel alive in its grotesque way.

I gag, forcing myself to look. What little light comes from the street casts shadows that stretch across the walls, twisting the horror into shapes that almost seem to move. My hands shake, so I force them into my pockets.

Mary Jane's pretty face is nearly gone. There's little left but bone. I make myself turn and leave the room, furious at myself for letting this happen.

Outside, Lena waits, and I grip her hand. "I'm going to take notes first," I say, my voice tight. "I'm going to write every detail. Then I'll get my boss."

She nods, understanding, and we stand together in the cold, knowing our work tonight has only just begun, and that Jack the Ripper is still out there.

# A LIFE LIKE THIS

## *LENA*

THE BREAKFAST TABLE between us is set with plates of food neither of us has touched. Mark sits opposite me, staring into his cup, undoubtedly torturing himself with the same question.

*How could we have let this happen?*

It's been two days since Mary Jane Kelly was murdered, two days since we sat outside her apartment while she was torn apart inside. I can't stop thinking about the quiet, how quiet it was until the Ripper stepped out the door and ran. We were so close, so damn close.

Mark hasn't spoken much since. He looks tired, and I know he blames himself, as do I.

"I kept thinking we'd see Kosminski being trailed by Finch and Briggs, and we'd just catch him trying to break into her apartment," I say.

"Somehow, Finch and Briggs got assigned a different shift that night. They switched with Parker and Clarke, who ignored my orders to trail Kosminski."

"Ignoring those orders is very suspicious, which is exactly what I'd expect from Parker and Clarke."

He clears his throat, his voice rough. "Lena, I was thinking... my mum lives in the country." His eyes meet mine. "She's got a little house near Surrey. It's a quiet place. I thought perhaps we could go for a few days, get away from all this."

"That sounds wonderful, Mark."

He nods. "We could both use a break from the city."

Relief mixed with guilt rushes through me. I don't deserve to feel lighter when Mary Jane's death still haunts me, but the thought of fresh air and open fields instead of fog-choked alleys makes my chest ache with longing.

"I'd love that."

He smiles for the first time in days. "Good. We'll leave this afternoon."

I nod, pushing back my chair. "I should tell Shannon where we're going."

He stands, too, adjusting his coat. "We can stop by The Ten Bells on our way out."

We move quietly around the small house, gathering our belongings. There's something surreal about packing for a journey to the countryside in another century.

Mark buckles the suitcase closed. "Are we ready?"

I nod, and we step out into the chilly morning. The streets glisten from last night's rain, and I grip Mark's arm as we walk.

The Ten Bells is warm and loud when we step inside, a sharp contrast to the damp cold outside. The smell of beer, sweat, and frying meat fills the air. Shannon is behind the bar, her hair tied up in a loose knot. When she spots us, I see worry in her eyes.

"Lena, love," she says, setting a mug down. "You look pale as a ghost. You two been sleeping at all?"

"Not much," I admit. "That's part of why we came. Mark's taking me out to the country for a few days to visit his mother."

Shannon glances at Mark as if seeking permission to tease him. "His *mother*, is it? Sounds proper enough." Then her expression sobers. "You'll both be happier away from here. This wretched city's cursed."

Mark leans on the counter. "Promise me you'll keep indoors after dark, you and your friends?"

"We will," Shannon says. "Not that there's much joy to be had out after sunset anymore." Her voice lowers, full of grief. "Poor Mary Jane."

I reach for her hand. "I know she was your friend. I'm so sorry, Shannon."

She nods. "Go on, then. Go get some peace while you can."

I hug her tightly. "We'll be back soon. Take care of yourself."

Outside, a light drizzle mists our faces as we make our way toward Whitechapel Station, and I can't shake the memory of the last time we were here. We were so close to the Ripper before he vanished on The Tube. Mark explained that the railway would be faster than taking a carriage all the way. The new line threads part of the city to the countryside, and after that, we'll take a hired carriage the rest of the way to his mother's home.

The train arrives with a roar, and I cling to Mark's arm as we step inside. Every lurch of the train underfoot makes my stomach churn. This is the same route the killer took to escape us, and now we are following it, creeping through the shadows of the very tunnels that swallowed him.

By the time we emerge into daylight again, the world feels transformed. The air is fresh and clean, scented by wet grass and earth, a startling contrast to the stench of filth and refuse that clings to the city streets, where human waste is tossed carelessly into alleys and backyards. It's a grotesque reality of something I had always read about in history books but never truly grasped until I lived it.

Rolling green fields stretch beyond the station, and the sky feels impossibly blue and wide. We take the small carriage for the final leg of the journey, the road winding through hedges and sheep herds until the cottage comes into view. It's a charming stone home with ivy clinging to its walls and smoke puffing lazily from the chimney.

Mark's mother is in her front yard tending to some flowers, and when she sees her son, her whole demeanor brightens. "Mark!" she calls, hurrying forward.

He grins, all the tension melting from him in an instant. "Hello,

Mum." He embraces her tightly and then turns to me. "Mum, this is Lena. She's a very good friend. I wanted you to meet her."

I smile proudly. "It's lovely to meet you, Mrs. Harrow."

"Please, call me Eleanor." She gestures toward the cottage. "Come in, both of you. You must be cold and hungry from the journey."

Inside, everything is warm and clean. Dried lavender hangs from the beams, and the scent of freshly baked bread wafts from the kitchen. Through the windows, I can see a small orchard and fields beyond, dotted with sheep and the shapes of distant workers tending to them.

"It's beautiful here," I say.

Eleanor smiles, starting tea. "This land has been in the Harrow family for generations. Mark's father farmed from the time he was a child, helping his father and grandfather. He worked this land all throughout our marriage, until the day he passed." Her voice trembles, but she doesn't dwell on the sorrow. "The farmhands help me with the fields now. They're good folks."

Mark sits beside me, visibly relaxing. His mother reaches across the table to pat his hand. "You've been working too much, my lad. Stay as long as you like, both of you."

I almost forget the grime, the blood, and the terror that hangs over London. Here, there's a comforting feeling of family.

THE NEXT MORNING DAWNS PINK AND ORANGE. BIRDS CHATTER IN THE bushes, and sunlight spills across Mark's childhood bedroom. He took the sofa so that his mother wouldn't be uncomfortable with the two of us sleeping in the same room. I dress and join him and his mother in the kitchen, where she insists on having tea before we go anywhere. Eleanor pours steaming cups of chamomile tea and fusses over the basket she's packed for us.

"It's such a gorgeous morning for some fresh air. I put in the good jam." She winks at me. "You'll want it when you find a sunny spot."

Mark laughs, standing, and kisses her cheek. "You've thought of everything, Mum."

She swats him playfully with her apron. "Go on before I put you to work cleaning out the cellar."

We walk hand in hand through the orchard. Beyond the trees, a small hill overlooks the fields, and we spread out a blanket there. The picnic basket holds fresh bread, butter, strawberry jam, a bit of cheese, and a bottle of elderflower cordial. Mark lies back, his hands folded behind his head, and stares at the November sky.

We eat, trade jokes, and tease each other. My cheeks hurt from laughter, which feels rare and precious. When he catches my hand and presses a kiss to my knuckles, peace spreads through me.

Later, we return to the cottage to visit with Eleanor. She tells stories about Mark as a boy, fondly remembering how he used to sneak biscuits from the pantry, how he tried to build a raft in the pond and nearly sank it with himself aboard, and how one Christmas he blamed the dog for a missing pie that he'd actually eaten. I laugh, and Mark looks at his mother with mock indignation.

"You're meant to protect my reputation, not destroy it." He shakes his head, but he's hiding a grin.

Eleanor just smiles. As the day fades, we decide to cook supper for her, preparing roasted chicken, vegetables, and fresh bread. Mark chops the vegetables while I bake the bread, and it all feels so easy and domestic. Eleanor hums softly in the next room, mending socks by lamplight.

By the time we sit down to eat, Mark decides to open a bottle of blackberry wine. It's all so mundane, and yet, it feels extraordinary after everything we've been through.

When Eleanor goes upstairs to bed early, Mark and I sit on the couch by the fire. He stretches his legs out, sipping the last of the wine, and I rest my head on his shoulder. I think of how safe I feel here and how rare that feeling is these days.

For a moment, I let myself imagine what life might be like if I stayed in this time. If we solve the case, would he leave London behind for the countryside? We could have a small cottage like this and spend our days walking through fields, and our evenings by the fire. Maybe I could almost forget about going back to the future. It feels as though the ache of not belonging could disappear out here with him....

But then I think of my mom and how she used to call just to ask me about my day. She always worried if I didn't answer right away. She'll never know what happened to me, that I'm alive somewhere she can't reach. The thought breaks my heart.

Mark brushes his hand over my cheek. "What are you thinking about?" he asks.

"My mom, mostly," I admit. "She must think I'm dead. Same with my aunt and uncle, my cousins... they all probably think I drowned in the Thames. I keep wondering what I'd give to have one more dinner together." I swallow hard.

He squeezes my hand gently, his thumb tracing my knuckles. "They must miss you terribly."

"I miss them," I whisper. "Every minute. But I also...." My voice trails off as I glance at him. "I think that I could get used to a life like this. It's so beautiful here."

He leans close, his lips brushing my neck, and I tilt my head back, trying to stifle a moan. Pleasure floods me, and I press into him, the thrill of closeness making me burn for him. Every touch makes me tingle, and I can feel the tension building between us.

His hands roam over me, teasing, and I try to stay quiet while the urgency between us grows. He slides his hand up my dress and drags his fingers up and down my folds until I'm writhing against him, my hands pressed over my mouth, fighting back the moans threatening to escape.

Silently, we move to his bedroom. I undo his pants, and his hard, throbbing cock springs free. I can't wait to feel him inside me. I stroke him, and he closes his eyes, letting out a quiet, satisfied groan.

Mark lays me back on the bed, pushes my dress up to my waist, and spreads my legs. He kisses up and down one thigh and then the other. The head of his cock slides against me, enticing me, but not entering me yet. When he reaches down to unbutton the top of my dress, my breasts pop out, and he teases my hard nipples before guiding himself inside of me with one smooth, long stroke.

I grab onto his biceps tightly, ecstasy flooding through me, every nerve alive with sensation. I can't get enough, can't hold back as he picks up the pace, harder and harder, until we both climax, caught up in the rush.

Finally, we collapse into each other, our bodies entwined. I let myself melt into the intensity of the moment, all the lust and longing colliding.

After a few moments, we begin to re-dress and compose ourselves. I glance over at him, and he's watching me with awe in his expression, and I can't help but blush again. "You are so extraordinarily beautiful," he says. "I will never grow tired of looking at you as long as I live."

I laugh, feeling pride, desire, and joy all at once. "You always know exactly what to say," I whisper, leaning into him. I realize I don't want this moment or this trip to end.

Just to be here, with him, feeling seen and wanted, is everything.

# PLAYGROUND OF TERROR

## *MARK*

THE COUNTRYSIDE FEELS like a dream I don't want to wake from. Lena and I spend our mornings wandering through the orchard, the sun warming our faces. The birdsong is so different from the clanging chaos of London it makes me never want to leave. Every meal with my mother feels like a glimpse of a world where the city's horrors can't reach us. I watch Lena laugh, the wind tossing her hair, and I try to freeze that moment forever.

But the real world waits. The memory of Mary Jane Kelly's body pulls relentlessly at the edges of my mind, a shadow I can't escape no matter how many fields we walk through or how many sunbeams fall across Lena's pretty face. I glance at the clock. The train back to London leaves in an hour, and I know we can't prolong our journey. Duty calls. Justice calls.

"I wish we could stay," Lena says quietly as we pack.

"Me, too," I admit. "But we can't. There's work waiting for me."

She nods, understanding, though I see the small crease of disappointment on her forehead. I hate that I'm dragging her back into the city when I know she loves it here.

My mum cries when I hug her goodbye, but she tells Lena she trusts her to look out for me. Lena says she will, and I believe her.

The train ride is quieter than before. We hold hands, but our conversation is sparse. London feels colder and smaller. When we arrive, I guide Lena to my house, doing my best to keep the sense of calm we had in the country alive for a few more minutes.

"I'll see you tonight," she says.

"I'll be home before you know it," I promise, brushing a curl from her face. "Just remember to lock the door."

She nods, and I walk away, leaving her watching me from the window.

At the office, my desk is cluttered with reports, and Finch and Briggs hover with worried expressions. Across the room, my boss, Chief Inspector Abberline, stares at me with his arms crossed, eyes narrowed, and jaw tight.

"Harrow," he says, approaching my desk. "Why was Kosminski your primary target? Montague John Druitt is our main suspect now. You've wasted valuable time chasing someone else."

I swallow hard, keeping my frustration in check. "I had Finch and Briggs following him, sir. There are patterns, eyewitness accounts, evidence, and leads that look promising. I thought it was our best chance of catching him in the act."

"You thought wrong," he snaps. "We can't afford mistakes like this. The investigation can't hinge on assumptions."

I nod, trying to mask the sting of disapproval as he walks back into his office. I return to my work. Montague John Druitt is now the main suspect, and every lead I thought worth pursuing with Kosminski is set aside.

I flip open Druitt's file, letting the pages spread across my desk like a map of his life and supposed crimes—birth records, employment details, timelines, witness statements, some corroborated, some contradictory. Each note feels flat and clearly lacks the spark that had drawn me to Kosminski. Still, this is my job. I absorb every detail, making mental notes of inconsistencies and overlaps. I compare dates and cross-reference locations in witness testimonies.

I notice there are more notes in Druitt's file from two particular constables than others. There's something off about the way Parker and Clarke have helped move this investigation along. They seem to be nudging the focus away from the tracks we need to follow. Framing Druitt could be convenient for them. My gut tells me there's more beneath the surface.

That evening, I pack up the file, tucking the papers carefully into my satchel, and head home. The scent of dinner greets me before I even step inside the house. Lena appears in the kitchen doorway, her hair piled loose, her apron dusted with flour.

"Mark." Smiling, she crosses the room.

I pull her into a long kiss, the weight of the day falling from my shoulders for a moment. She laughs, pressing her hands against my chest before I set down my bag.

"Dinner smells delicious," I murmur.

"You must be starving. Come on, sit."

After we eat, I spread Druitt's file across the table. I summarize the official case: his movements, the timeline, the letters and reports. Lena leans in, her eyes focused as she studies the pictures and descriptions.

"I don't think it's him," she says finally, her voice steady. "I think it's Kosminski. The man we chased—his eyes, the way he moved—it's burned into me. I recognize him, Mark."

I study her face, the certainty in her eyes. It matches my own lingering instincts. "But in all these files, the evidence points to Druitt."

"Maybe it's not about what's in the files," she says. "Look at the way Parker and Clarke have pushed this. It doesn't sit right. I think they're trying to frame Druitt. Maybe they've got a hand in more than just falsifying a suspect."

I feel a spark of agreement, the familiar rush of purpose returning. We pore over the documents together, comparing timelines, sightings, and inconsistencies. Slowly, piece by piece, the outlines of a dangerous deception begin to emerge.

The next morning, I walk into the office and head straight for Abberline. His door is open, with papers scattered across his desk. He doesn't look up immediately, his pen scratching across a report.

I clear my throat. "Sir, may I have a word?"

He glances up, his eyes sharp. "Make it quick, Harrow."

"It's about Druitt. I've gone over the file in detail, cross-referenced every statement, every alibi. The more I dig, the less it adds up. His timelines are convenient, but there's nothing concrete linking him to the murders. And yet—" I pause, weighing my words carefully, "Kosminski fits the profile, the man we followed. His behavior, the nervous energy, the way he moves, his mental instability–there's a pattern. I think he's our killer."

Abberline leans back, frowning. "You think because you tailed him for a few days, and he did absolutely nothing illegal, that we should ignore every other suspect? That's reckless, Harrow. Druitt is the one with motive, with opportunity, according to the records."

"I understand that," I say, keeping my tone even. "But the facts on Druitt are tidy because someone wanted them to be. It feels too convenient, sir. Parker and Clarke have been steering this investigation hard toward Druitt. It's possible that they're framing him. Perhaps they've got reasons to misdirect the case entirely. I've noticed inconsistencies in their reports and behavior that don't make sense otherwise."

"Harrow, that is far beyond speculation. You're treading on dangerous ground, implying our own men are manipulating evidence. If you can't keep your theories anchored in fact, I will relieve you of this case."

I feel the blood drain from my face but refuse to look away. "Sir, I'm not suggesting this lightly. I'm saying the evidence points to someone else, and there's reason to believe Druitt is being used as a convenient scapegoat. We owe it to the victims to follow the leads where they actually point."

Abberline stands abruptly, slamming a hand on the desk. "Enough. You follow the investigation as it is laid out. Focus on Druitt, document everything properly, and do it by the book. No more chasing shadows or personal hunches. Step out of line again, and you're off this case entirely. Do I make myself clear?"

"Yes, sir," I reply, my voice tight. The fight drains from me, replaced by a gnawing frustration. I want to argue, to tell him he's missing the real patterns, but I know this isn't the time or the place.

When I get home, I'm still thinking about Abberline's warning. I unlock the door and push it open, already loosening my tie.

"Lena?" I call out.

She's looking out the window, pale and teary-eyed. "Mark," she says, voice catching. "He's been here."

My heart stops. "What do you mean?"

She holds out a letter. "He slid it under the door," she whispers.

I take it from her and unfold it carefully. The familiar handwriting leaps out.

*Dear Gov,*

*You're not too quick are you? You wait for me, but I'm already home. You run in circles while I walk free.*

*The lady at your house, she's a fine one. If I can't have her, I'll make do with the red bird she shops with.*

*Yours truly,*

*Jack the Ripper*

I can't breathe. His cruel, mocking, sick sort of humor makes my blood boil.

Lena's voice shakes. "He means Shannon. He's been following her, Mark. You know he has."

I look up. "When was this delivered?"

"Minutes before you came home. I heard the paper slide under the door, and I've been staring out the window ever since."

I glance toward the window, my pulse hammering. The street outside looks the same, but every shadow feels dangerous. "All right," I say, forcing calm. "We're not panicking. We'll think this through."

She nods, though her hands won't stop trembling. "It's him, Mark. It's Kosminski."

I spread the letter flat on the table beside the other files. "It does sound like him," I admit. "The phrasing. It's the kind of thing that tumbles out of a fractured mind."

I read the lines again, slower this time, the taunting tone, the fixation on Lena and Shannon. He loves goading me, and he's made this personal. He's hunting us.

Lena's voice drops to a whisper. "We have to warn Shannon. Tonight."

"We will," I promise, gathering the letter and sliding it into a file. "I'll have Finch and Briggs keep watch over her."

I hate him. I hate the way he turns the city into his playground of terror, the way he shreds bodies and lives like they're nothing. He wrote this letter because he wants me furious enough to make a mistake.

I will not give him the satisfaction.

# RED BIRD

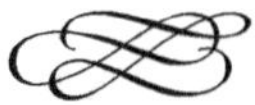

## *LENA*

MARK PULLS a revolver out of a drawer and slams it shut. "We're not walking tonight," he says, his voice low and tense. "Not after that letter. We'll take a cab."

I look out the window and fidget with the buttons on my coat. "The streets seem darker tonight."

"They're certainly not safe," Mark says. "We need to get to the station without risking our lives. No shortcuts and no alleys."

I follow him outside, the cold night air biting at my cheeks. Mark whistles for a hansom cab, and one pulls up. He helps me in and then climbs in beside me, his eyes scanning the streets as if he expects Kosminski to appear around the next corner.

The cab jolts as the horse moves. I keep my voice quiet. "Do you really think Finch and Briggs will—"

"They'll do what I tell them," Mark interrupts. "They don't have a choice. Shannon's life depends on it."

The cab stops in front of the station, and Mark helps me down, keeping one hand near his gun. He strides into the building, and I follow. We find two cops getting their coats and whistles on, readying themselves for the night shift.

"Finch, Briggs," Mark says, his tone serious. "Tonight you're both trailing Shannon, the redhead that works at The Ten Bells. Keep her safe. She's being threatened by the killer."

Just then, an older man in a crisp uniform, the insignia marking him clearly above Mark in rank, strides into the room. His eyes narrow as they sweep over us. "Harrow," he says. "I've heard enough. Why are you having them follow some whore around? You're far too close to this. Emotion is clouding your judgment."

Mark's hands tighten around the letter as he unfolds it. "Abberline, sir, with respect—" He holds up the paper. "You need to see this. The barmaid is in danger. This isn't just conjecture."

Abberline takes the letter and scans the red ink. "You're suspended," Abberline says, his voice sharp and final. "Effective immediately. You need to get completely out of town, Harrow. You're compromising the investigation. This monster clearly has a problem with you and with the women you have hanging about." His eyes move to me, filled with disdain, and I feel the weight of his judgment as if he's peering straight through me.

Mark steps forward, his voice fierce. "These women are in danger! This isn't just a case! These women's lives are at stake!"

Abberline doesn't waver. "That's precisely why you're being removed. You must recuse yourself, Harrow. Step aside."

Mark's jaw tightens, and I see his hands tremble slightly, not with fear, but with the rage and the helplessness he's fighting to control.

We step out of the station and immediately scan the street. Mark drops his hand to my back, comforting me. "We don't have time to wait," he says.

I nod, the urgency in his voice matching my fear. We find another hansom cab, and though we move quickly, the city feels like a trap tonight, every shadow a potential threat.

The cab stops outside The Ten Bells. We leap down, our boots splashing through puddles. Mark's hand brushes mine as we sprint up the steps, fumbling for the door. Inside, the familiar murmur of voices greets us.

Louisa and Flossie are behind the bar, polishing glasses, glancing up as we enter. "Where's Shannon?" I ask, approaching the bar.

"She stepped out back," Louisa says casually. "Went out to take the rubbish, like she usually does. Said she'd be right back."

My stomach churns. "Outside?" I whisper.

"Yes," Louisa nods. "She's fine, love. Right out the back door."

We burst through the backdoor out into the night–and then I see her.

Shannon is lying on the cold stone street, her body still, twisted in the pale glow of moonlight. My stomach drops, bile rising, and I stumble forward, but Mark's hand catches my arm, holding me back.

I can barely breathe. The sight is more than grief. It claws at my chest, steals the air. Her throat is slit, her abdomen cruelly slashed, and blood stains the stones around her, vivid and raw against the dark alley. On the wall behind her, in thick, dripping letters, he has written: **RED BIRD.**

My legs shake so violently I can barely hold myself up. "Mark," I whisper. My voice cracks. "Oh, God...."

He doesn't answer me. He's already working, crouched beside her, his notebook in hand, recording, measuring with meticulous precision. Every instinct honed over years of detective work is in overdrive. He ignores the fear, the suspension, the danger. Even now, even though Abberline wanted him away from this, he documents every detail like a man possessed.

"Lena," he says, quietly but firmly, without looking up. "Go inside. Tell your friends not to come out here. No one goes out. Understand?"

I want to scream, to run, to grab him and collapse into him, but I obey. I take a step back, my body rigid, my stomach twisting. Every breath is painful.

I stagger back inside, shutting the door hard behind me as if I can block out the pain. Louisa and Flossie both look up from behind the bar, concern carved into their faces.

"Stay inside," I manage, my voice shaking. "Whatever happens, don't go out back. Don't go anywhere."

Flossie looks scared. "What's wrong, love?"

I shake my head, my throat closing up. "Please," I beg. "Just… stay here."

They exchange a worried glance, but I can't bear to explain. My legs give out, so I sink onto a barstool. The room sways. I press my fingertips over my eyes, trying to breathe, trying not to picture what I just saw.

Flossie comes closer, her voice trembling. "Lena, you're frightening us. What's happened?"

Before I can answer, the front door swings open behind me. Two uniformed constables step in. I recognize them from before: Finch and Briggs. They look around the pub.

I stand on unsteady legs and cross over to them, wiping the tears from my cheeks. "I didn't think you were coming," I say, my voice rough from crying.

Briggs frowns. "We weren't supposed to," he admits. "But Finch here had a gut feeling we should check on the maiden tonight. Couldn't shake it."

I stare at them for a long moment, then the words pour out of me before I can stop them. "Well, you were too late." My voice cracks. "She's already gone."

Both men freeze, the meaning sinking in. "Gone?" Finch asks.

"She's dead." The words scrape out of my throat. "Out back. Harrow's there now, documenting the scene. He told me to come inside and to keep everyone away."

Behind me, Louisa screams. Flossie lets out a gasp, her hand flying to her mouth. The glass she'd been polishing slips from her fingers and shatters on the floor.

I sink back onto the stool, trembling, trying to breathe through the guilt that is choking me. I can feel the tears starting again, spilling down my face.

Staring at the empty doorway to the kitchen, I imagine Shannon with her bright hair and pretty smile, carrying a tray of mugs. I should have stopped her. I should have been here to protect her. Better yet, if I hadn't traveled back in time and changed history, she would be alive right now.

"We need to fetch the Chief Inspector," Finch says behind me.

"He must see this at once," Briggs replies.

I hear them move toward the door, their boots clicking against the floor. I sit back down at the bar, my head bowed, silent. I don't know what they're planning, nor do I care. Shannon is gone. I should go warn Mark that his boss is on the way, but I can't move. Shannon is dead.

I have no idea how much time has passed when Abberline steps through the door, his expression cold. He's flanked by Finch and Briggs. Without a word, they move toward the back door. I rise instinctively and follow, careful to keep my distance.

Mark is crouched next to Shannon, still taking notes. Abberline stops a few feet behind him. "Inspector Harrow," he says. "You have repeatedly ignored orders. Effective immediately, you are no longer an officer of Scotland Yard. You are to have no further involvement in this case or any others."

Mark steps forward, his voice laced with fury. "This woman's blood is on your hands, Abberline! I warned you. I know who did this! It was Kosminski, and yet you did nothing! She is dead because of your inaction!"

Finch and Briggs move forward and firmly guide Mark away from their boss. I follow him through the bar and out the front, moving quickly to keep up. He hails a cab, and we climb in.

I press myself against the side of the carriage, wishing I could vanish, and wishing I were anywhere but here. Every shadow reminds me that Kosminski is still out there, hunting us, and that he's coming for me next. My heart aches with grief for Shannon, the friend I couldn't save, and with every passing block, this world feels suffocating and hostile.

I want to go home, to my own time, where none of this exists, where Jack the Ripper can't follow me, and where I'm safe.

# TRUTH HURTS

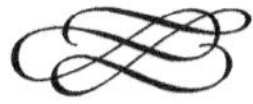

## *MARK*

W E   MAKE  it to my house fast, and I pay the driver, quickly pulling Lena through the door. The bolt slides home with a hard click. I run around the house, checking every window and latch, keeping the revolver with me.

Lena sinks onto the couch, her shoulders trembling. I sit beside her, resting my hand on her back. "I should have comforted you back there," I admit. "I wanted to get every detail at the scene while I could, but I should've held you."

"It's all right," she whispers, burying her face in my chest.

I cradle the back of her head, fingers tangling in her hair as she sobs. Holding her closer, I let her grief pour into me. "I'm so sorry, Lena." We sit like that for a long moment. I can't help the guilt clawing at me, the weight of every failure and every life lost. "If only we'd been there earlier. I would've taken out the rubbish. He could've fought with me instead of Shannon."

Lena shakes her head violently against me. "No. You did everything you could. It's not your fault. It's him. Kosminski, Jack the Ripper." Her voice breaks again, raw and ragged. "I should have warned her better. I should have—"

I pull her tighter, pressing my lips to her forehead. "No. None of this is your fault."

Her sobs continue, filled with desperation, and I try to steady her shaking shoulders. "We survived," I whisper. "We live to stop him. We can't change what's done, but we can make sure it doesn't happen again. We can sit here and mourn all night, or we can do something."

She swallows hard, sniffing, and nods. "You're right. We have to keep trying. We have work to do."

"Kosminski's always one step ahead, always gone before we can even—" I stop, running a hand through my hair. "How does he vanish so easily? The train station, the alleys, even the river twice–he's always gone before we can touch him."

Lena's gaze lifts from her notes. "That's what I've been thinking," she says. "Mark, what if he's like me? What if he's not bound by time?"

I freeze mid-step. "You mean he's jumping through time to keep from getting caught? Lena, that doesn't really make a lot of sense. There are other ways he could be getting away from us so quickly."

"I know it sounds crazy, but so is the fact that I'm here, out of my own time and stuck in yours. If that can happen to me, why couldn't it happen to him? What if Kosminski's a time traveler, too?"

I stare at her. "Because, Lena, you did it once. You're saying he's coming and going as he pleases. That seems much less plausible."

She shrugs. "True. How do we explain how he vanishes into the river, and why there's no trace afterward?"

I pace a few more steps, thinking. "The Thames is famous for keeping bodies hidden, Lena. It keeps killers hidden as well. You know how dark the streets are and how quickly he can get to the train." Exhaustion and grief are clouding her thinking.

"I know of other killers from the future, people who fit the same pattern as Jack the Ripper," Lena says. She spreads sheets of paper across the table and starts jotting down names, places, and the decades they operated in. "I've seen documentaries, written papers and studied case files about them. I don't remember exact dates or times, just the general periods, where they were, and the kinds of victims they targeted. If we lay it all out, maybe we can see if any of it connects to Kosminski."

I lean in, curious. "Show me."

"Peter Kürten," she begins, writing his name at the top. "The Vampire of Düsseldorf, Germany. He targeted women and children. He stabbed or mutilated his victims, and he had sexual motives mixed with extreme sadism. He operated just like Kosminski, but about forty years later."

She writes down the next name. "H. H. Holmes. He was in Chicago, 1890s. He had secret torture chambers in his home, which was dubbed The Murder Castle. He killed mostly vulnerable women for sexual reasons."

"Germany? Chicago?" I ask, skepticism sharpening my tone. "Those places are thousands of miles away."

"Distance doesn't mean anything to him," she says. "If he can move through time, he has no problem traveling continents."

She writes another name. "Jack Unterweger. Austria, 1970s until the 1990s, I believe. He, too, targeted sex workers, but he strangled them. He also left bodies for the public to find instead of disposing of or burying them. His name is even Jack. The signature changes slightly, but the essence remains. Kosminski, Jack the Ripper. He could be all of them."

My mind spins. "Do you remember what any of those men look like? Do any of them look like Kosminski?"

"No, but Jack the Ripper, whoever he is, could be adapting identities. That could be why nothing ever completely connects. He moves, changes his appearance, and disappears before a trail can form."

"If what you're suggesting is true, we're not dealing with a man," I say. "We're dealing with a force, something that transcends time. Honestly, Lena, I don't think it's likely."

"You're probably right." She drags a hand through her hair. "Maybe I'm losing my mind."

"No, you're exhausted, and nothing else is making sense." I pat her shoulder and stare down at the stack of crime scene photographs spread across the coffee table, and one in particular makes me look twice–the first victim, Polly Nichols, posing for a photo her sister provided us with for her file. I've looked at this picture a dozen times, but tonight, something new catches my eye: a brooch on her collar.

I lean closer, using the magnifying glass. The pin is small and oval-shaped, and the pattern carved into it is unmistakable, a curling vine looping around a single stone. I glance toward Lena, sitting on the edge of the couch, still writing down notes. The same brooch gleams at her collar.

"Lena, where did you get that brooch?"

"I found it back in my time. I was mudlarking in the Thames," she whispers. "I saw this brooch just lying there in the mud. I pinned it to my shirt moments before I fell into the water."

I look back at the photograph. "Polly Nichols is wearing the same brooch. Lena, that can't be a coincidence."

She unpins the brooch. "Turn it over," she says. I flip it and read the name: **Polly.**

"Sometimes, I wonder if it's what pulled me back," she explains. "Maybe it has some kind of energy in it, something that connects me to your time."

The idea sounds bloody mad, but so does everything about her being here. "I wonder if the brooch could send you home?"

Her eyes search mine. "Maybe. If it brought me here, maybe it could take me back."

"You could be safe there. Away from all this. Away from him."

"Safe? I live in New York City in 2025. There are far worse villains than Jack the Ripper, and you wouldn't be there to protect me."

"As much as I want to protect you forever, I think you'd be safer back home. The truth hurts, but we both know you don't belong here."

She brushes her fingers over the brooch again. "Maybe I'm here for a reason. Maybe I'm supposed to help you solve this case. I think about going home every day, but then I look at you, and I don't want to leave."

We stay up for hours after that, the room filled with the rustle of papers and the scratch of Lena's pen. We jot down possible connections between killers throughout time and draw lines between names, years, and cities. Both of us think we are grasping at straws now, but studying other killers might lend a clue even if the Ripper is not a time traveler–and I honestly don't believe he is. Outside, London is silent except for the occasional clatter of a carriage on the street.

Lena yawns. "It's almost dawn," she murmurs. "We should stop before our eyeballs fall out."

She's right. My eyelids feel heavy, and my thoughts are dull from grief and regret. I push the papers aside and stack the photographs neatly. "We'll pick up again tomorrow."

Lena trails me down the short hall.

"You should take the side by the wall," I say. "It feels safer there."

She nods and slips beneath the blanket. I turn down the lamp, the darkness closing in. Lying beside her, staring at the ceiling, sleep doesn't come. My mind won't stop. Every time I close my eyes, I see Shannon's face.

Lena shifts closer, sound asleep, and I should find comfort in it, but instead, there's fear. The thought of losing her gnaws at me. Losing her to the Ripper or losing her to time itself.

If that brooch could send her back, shouldn't I want it to? She'd be safer in her own time, finally free from the blood of Whitechapel. But if she can go back–couldn't he, too? He could follow her home.

I watch her sleep as the glow from the streetlamp catches her hair and falls over her beautiful face. I reach out, my fingers stopping just short of her cheek, and whisper, "I won't let him take you."

# MUDLARKING

## *LENA*


WHEN I AWAKEN, the room is quiet. Mark lies beside me, still asleep, his arm across my waist. For a moment, I just watch him breathe, the rhythm proof that we've both made it through another day. I glance at the clock on the wall; it's half past 2:00 in the afternoon.

I slide carefully from beneath the blanket, trying not to wake him. His revolver sits on the nightstand, within reach even in sleep. Moving through the room quietly, I head for the kitchen, where I set the kettle on the stove and rummage through what little food we have. There's bread, a bit of cheese, eggs, and a few potatoes that haven't gone soft yet.

As the kettle begins to hiss, I peek out the window. The street outside looks empty, but that doesn't mean he isn't hiding nearby.

I turn back to the counter and slice the bread. The knife cuts through the loaf while my mind races. Too many have already died, and if we don't act, there will be more. Mark keeps talking about evidence and proof, but proof won't stop a killer who vanishes before we can reach him.

My plan's still half-formed, but it's there, waiting, solidifying with every second, and part of me knows Mark will hate it when I share it with him.

I hear movement behind me, the creak of the floorboards, then the splash of water. I follow the sound to the small washroom. He's at the basin, toothbrush in hand, his shirt open at the collar and his hair a mess.

I move behind him and run my fingers through his hair, and he freezes, his eyes lifting to meet mine in the mirror.

I smile, brushing a lock away from his temple. "I have an idea," I say.

He lowers the toothbrush, wary already. "That look on your face makes me nervous."

"I think you need a haircut."

That gets him. He frowns, curiosity in his eyes. "A haircut?"

"Yes." I cross my arms, leaning against the doorframe. "From Kosminski. I want you to go to his shop, act casual, see how he behaves. If he's hiding something, you'll see it."

He rinses his mouth and wipes his hands on a towel. "You want me to walk into the lion's den for a shave and trim?"

"Something like that."

We walk into the kitchen and sit down at the table to eat breakfast. "There's more," I say. "You'll take either Finch or Briggs with you, and while you're there, mention, very casually, that your bird likes to go mudlarking at dusk by the Thames. Plan the conversation ahead of time so that it flows naturally."

Mark's fork clatters against the plate. "Absolutely not. That's a terrible idea. You're not going anywhere near the river, not if he's out there."

"Mark," I say quietly, leaning forward. "He's going to kill again. If we wait for the police or conclusive evidence, more women will die. I'm not letting that happen."

He shakes his head. "You're not going to be bait."

"You need to help me because I'm doing it whether you help or not."

His eyes meet mine, storm-dark and furious, but I don't look away. I wear him down one argument at a time. Every time he says no, I say his name softly and remind him that we're running out of time, that Shannon deserves justice.

"You're the only one who can do this," I tell him.

"It's madness," he mutters. "Walking into his shop, sitting down in front of him like nothing's wrong—"

"He's not going to kill you in broad daylight or in public. You're just a man getting a haircut," I say. "That's all it is. You sit, you watch, you mention me to one of your constables, nothing more."

He runs a hand through his hair, grimacing at the idea. "And I'm not even employed by Scotland Yard anymore, so how am I supposed to get one of those constables to do that?"

"Those two are different. They want to help; I can tell. And Mark, I'm so sorry you lost your job over this. I know how much your career meant to you."

A long silence stretches between us before he sighs and grabs his coat from the hook. "Lock the door. Keep the gun with you. I'll be back soon."

The door shuts, and I'm alone. The house is too quiet. I light a lamp and check all the windows twice. After I get dressed, I pace for a long time. My hands shake when I finally pour water from the kettle into a cup for tea. I sit at the kitchen table, keeping the revolver beside me.

Somewhere down the street, a man yells, and I flinch. I picture Mark sitting in the barber chair, Kosminski behind him with scissors glinting in the light.

I don't know how much time passes before footsteps sound on the stoop. I look out the window and see Mark unlocking the door. "It's done," he says, stepping inside. "Finch and I both got our hair cut by a vicious killer, and we set the trap. It took all my will power not to kill him with his own shears."

I don't even realize I'm moving until I'm in his arms. The relief crashes over me. I kiss him–deep and desperate. He kisses me back with a raw mix of fear, sorrow, and relief.

We stumble toward the bedroom, our hands finding buttons, his boots thudding to the floor. Clothes fall in a messy heap around us as the tension between us ignites. I climb onto the bed, straddling him and sliding down until he's buried deep within me.

He groans and reaches up to tease my breasts as I find my rhythm. I lean back to feel him as deeply as possible. I moan from the pleasure. He slides his hand down my body, leaving a trail of heat.

I build momentum, and we both lose ourselves in the moment.

"Slow down," he whispers. "I don't want this to be over so quickly."

I obey, leaning forward to press my lips to his. He kisses me and rolls me over gently, pulling me close from behind. The intensity of his touch takes my breath away, and I almost climax from the first stroke.

When he leans down, his lips brush my ear, and he whispers, "I love you."

Heat surges through me, and together, we reach our peak, breathless and burning with desire. He moves off me and lies down beside me.

I press my hand to his chest. "I love you, too," I whisper. In this moment, nothing else matters, just us.

I picture us on the other side of this, finally free of the killer, and finally able to breathe without looking over our shoulders. I force myself to hold on to the small, stubborn hope that we'll catch him and survive, that maybe we'll get to have a life together after all this.

But the thought won't leave me: tonight could be it. *I could die.* My stomach turns over at the thought, but I push the fear down. I can't let fear freeze me now.

Still, I think of my mom, and how she'll never know what really happened to me. I fight back tears thinking about how she probably thinks I'm already dead, and they probably already had my funeral. I miss my mom so much it hurts sometimes, but I can't go back yet, not until this is finished.

Or maybe not at all… because somewhere along the way, I fell in love.

THE SKY BLEEDS BLUE, GRAY, AND VIOLET AS THE SUN SINKS BEHIND THE rooftops, the river slick and oil black. I crouch near the water's edge, pretending to sift through the mud for trinkets. I hold a lantern, which throws a wavering pool of light over my boots and the rolling tide.

Mark is hidden somewhere behind the wall of the embankment, just beyond the curve where the river bends. He's about fifty feet away, maybe less. He'd wanted to be closer, but there was no way that would work. He'd be too exposed. The open stretch of bank means he'd be seen before the killer even showed himself. So he waits in the shadows, his revolver in hand, ready for a sound, a signal, a scream.

Every ripple of water sounds like footsteps. Every creak of wood from the distant docks makes my heart leap. The fog rolls in low and fast, swallowing the far side of the river. I keep my eyes down, searching for some gleam in the muck, pretending I'm not the bait.

Then, I hear the sound of boots on sand coming from the darkness upriver.

I can't breathe.

A figure emerges from the fog, moving with a slow, predatory gait. He wears a long coat and a hat pulled low, the lower half of his face hidden by a handkerchief. He's closer than Mark is, and every step makes my stomach drop. My blood freezes, and I know that if he reaches me, I'm done.

"Good evening," he says, his voice muffled. "You play your part well, miss."

My mouth goes dry. "I don't know what you mean."

He tilts his head, the edge of a smile beneath the cloth. "Oh, I think you do. You're the decoy, aren't you? But that's all right." He takes a step closer. "Your lover's out here somewhere, I know. Watching, waiting to play the hero."

I glance toward where Mark is hiding and pray he can see me clearly through the mist.

"He can watch," the man continues. "I don't care who sees. That's how badly I want you."

Panic rips through me. I know he's going to kill me. I scream for

Mark, spin around to run, but the Ripper's already there, lunging. His hand clamps over my arm, dragging me back. I kick and struggle, trying to break free, and my hands dart to his face. I rip at the handkerchief, pulling it down. Finally, I see him fully.

Kosminski.

We stumble toward the riverbank, slipping on the wet mud, the edge of the shoreline crumbling beneath us, the bank giving way beneath our feet.

A gunshot cracks the air, the sound splitting through me as we fall. Kosminski's weight slams into me, and I see the knife before the river swallows us both. Cold water rips the breath from my lungs. I twist and kick, but he grabs me by my hair, dragging my face under.

Bubbles burst from my mouth as I thrash, tasting mud. The blade skims my side in a sharp, searing line that lights up my ribs. Blood spills into the water, the current turning sickly red.

Everything blurs until all light fades away.

# WHAT'S NEXT?

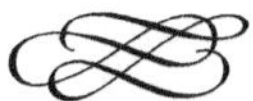

***Mark***

I see them tumble into the river, Lena thrashing in his grip, water churning around them. The Ripper's knife glints, slicing toward her, and my blood runs cold.

I sprint through the mud, knowing I have to reach her before the current drags her under or that bastard strikes again. The river roars in my ears, masking her screams, and all I can focus on is getting to her, diving in without a second thought, my arms ready to grab, pull, and protect.

"Hold on!" I roar, lunging for her.

I grab her wrist as the current yanks at her. She thrashes, gasping, water rushing around us. I force her against me, bracing against the river, trying to keep her from being swept under.

The Ripper lunges for Lena. He's bleeding heavily from my gunshot. I drive my boot into his chest, sending him tumbling back into the water, and then he's completely gone. One moment he's there, the next... he's vanished.

I spin, searching. Lena is under me, sinking. I grab her under her arms, holding her tight, trying to keep her above the water. The river pulls at us. I kick with everything left in me, each stroke a battle, each wave a threat.

I twist, pulling her closer, feeling the undertow tug at my boots and tear at my coat. We're swallowed by darkness, the night sky and murky water blending, each gasp for air a fight. I can't let go, can't lose her here, not like this.

The Ripper is gone, and yet the water is relentless. My limbs burn as I force a stroke, a kick, anything, to keep us afloat, but it's no use. The river is too strong, and the Thames takes us.

SOMEONE PULLS ME UPWARD, AND WHEN I BREAK THE SURFACE, MY chest explodes. I gulp air, coughing violently. I am shoved toward something solid, and I realize my boots are scraping against the side of a boat. When I'm shoved inside, I collapse against the wooden floor, shivering and gasping, trying desperately to catch my breath.

A second man hauls Lena up. She breaks the surface, coughing and sucking in air, and he fights the current to drag her toward the boat. I scramble to help lift her inside as relief punches through the terror.

*She's alive.*

I sink against the side of the boat, shaking, trying to get enough air to even think.

One of the men wipes water from his face, eyeing us with a mix of irritation and disbelief. "What in the devil's name were you two doing swimming out in this current? We saw you struggling and thought you'd be drowned before we could make it over to you. And that other fellow... what happened to him?"

I cough, still trying to pull air into my lungs. "Thank you for helping us. We... we weren't swimming. Someone was after us, trying to kill us."

The other fisherman shakes his head, water dripping from his beard. "Well, you got lucky, that's all I can say. One second he was there, the next he had disappeared downstream. We were just fishing, minding our own business, and now we're soaked hauling you two out."

Lena looks at the fishermen, her voice shaking. "You lost track of him?"

"He was there and then he went around the bend," the man clarifies. "Hopefully, he made it to shore. Come on, we'll get you to shore. Only thing we can do for you now."

When we step onto solid ground, I grip one of the fishermen's hands firmly. "Thank you. We owe you our lives."

"Don't mention it," he grunts.

Lena and I walk away, soaked and shivering, leaving them behind. I wrap my arms around her shaking body and hold her for several minutes, trying to catch my breath. She almost died—I almost lost her.

She lifts her head to look at me, but her eyes catch on something behind me. For a moment, I think she's spotted the Ripper again, but her tone isn't frightened—it's shocked.

"Mark… look around." Her eyes dart over the buildings, the streets, the metal and glass that glints in the morning sun.

I swallow hard, scanning the scene. The riverbank looks familiar, but everything else is wrong. "Where the hell are we?" I mutter.

"I… I think it's the year 2025," Lena says. "This is Whitechapel, but everything's the way it was when I left."

Some of the buildings look similar to the way I remember them, their brick faces worn yet familiar, but others are larger, smooth, and shiny, their walls reflecting the light in ways I've never seen. Strange shapes move along the wider, smoother streets like huge metal boxes.

The people look nothing like what I'm used to. Women wear trousers and jackets, their hair cut short or dyed colors like pink and blue. The clothes are tighter, brighter, some in strange shapes and styles I don't recognize at all. Even here in Whitechapel, where I know the streets, their clothing, these buildings—it all makes the place feel foreign, like I've stepped into another world.

I shake my head. "It can't be. How is this possible?"

"I don't know how you came with me. Maybe it was Polly's

brooch? Maybe when the Thames sucked me back to this year, I pulled the two of you along with me"

My mind races. "And the Ripper?" I ask. "What do you think happened to him?"

She glances around. "I don't know. I hope he drowned, but if he managed to pull himself out of the river, this isn't over."

I look around but don't see any sign of him. With a sigh, I say, "I bet you are ready to see your family."

Lena's eyes brim with tears. "Of course, but first I think I should find out how much time has passed since the day I fell in the river. I wish I knew what the exact date is today. If only I had my phone. I could just call my mom, my cousins… let's just find a place to get dry first."

I nod. We start cautiously, walking down the street. People stare. I notice their eyes on our soaked clothing, which must appear strange to them.

"We need to go somewhere we can think and get our bearings. A hotel, maybe?" I ask.

"That's a good idea, but we don't have any money."

"Perhaps we can make a temporary trade," I say, and she nods, understanding instantly. "Do you have anything of value?"

"I have my grandfather's pocket watch," I say. I don't want to let go of it, but if it helps Lena, I'll do whatever it takes.

We find the nearest inn on Cable Street. The clerk stares at us like we've jumped out of a painting, his arms crossed. I open my mouth, but Lena steps forward first, speaking quickly. "We fell in the river," she says. "We were on a riverboat doing a reenactment last night. We don't have any money with us, but this is a genuine Victorian relic."

She nods at me, and I take out my grandfather's pocket watch. The clerk frowns, reaching for a magnifying glass from a drawer. He examines the piece carefully, turning it over in his hands. Finally, he looks up. "This is real," he says. "But you're probably going to want it back, right?"

Lena and I exchange a glance. "Yes," she says. "Definitely. You can keep them until we get our wallets."

He nods, still eyeing the pieces with suspicion, then waves us toward a room. "Fine. One night. Don't make a mess."

We take the key and walk to the room. I pull the door closed behind us and lean against it for a moment. Lena is beside me, still dripping and shivering. I pull off my wet clothes, tossing them over a chair. Lena does the same, her damp hair clinging to her back. The bed is soft and inviting, and we collapse onto it together, exhaustion dragging us down.

Her body is chilled against me. She winces slightly when she shifts, and I notice a thin red line across her ribs. My heart lurches.

"Lena," I murmur, brushing my fingers gently over it. The cut is shallow, just a graze from his knife in the river, but it makes my blood boil with anger.

I kiss it softly. She lets out a small laugh, shaking her head. "It's not that bad." But I can see the memory of the fight in her eyes.

We lie there, the trauma of the fight with Jack in the river and traveling through time overwhelming, and yet it's comforting to be here with her.

"I have an idea," Lena says as she rises gracefully, every movement lithe and beautiful, the curve of her shoulders and the sway of her hips impossible to look away from. She moves toward the corner of the room and slips on a robe before fiddling with a black box sitting on a dresser. "Don't worry," she says over her shoulder, her voice calm. "It's going to turn on. There'll be a light and people talking inside it."

I swallow hard, my chest tight. "People... inside of it? Trapped somehow?"

She shakes her head, a playful smile tugging at her lips. "No, just watch." She presses a button, and the box comes to life, a bright glow spreading across the screen. Figures appear, moving and speaking, their lips matching the voices that fill the room. "By God... what manner of devilry is this?"

She glances at me. "It's a TV. It shows the news, among other things. People still have newspapers and other ways of getting the news, but most watch it on TV now." She points to the top of the screen. "See that? That's the date and time."

I stare, trying to wrap my mind around it.

"It's only the day after," she says, surprised and happy as she lies back down beside me. "The day after I fell into the water in 2025. Only a day has passed for my mom, my cousins, and my aunt and uncle." Relief floods her face. "That means they probably thought I drowned, but it's only been a day. I can call them later."

I nod, pulling her closer, my hands roaming her back. "We've survived everything. We're together, and we're safe."

"And you shot him, Mark. He's gone. Drowned or died from your gunshot."

I take her hand. "I think you're right. I don't see any sign of him here. It's over."

She shifts slightly, looking up at me. "But aren't you going to miss the past? Your mother? Your life there?"

I shrug, thoughts of my mother tugging at my heart. Still, she's more important. "I just want to be here with you. Nothing else matters right now."

I pull her closer, feeling her breath even out as she relaxes. We lie there in the quiet room, warm, safe and together, letting the adrenaline fade.

We talk about what comes next, about her family, and about how I'll adjust to this new world. I hold her, and for the first time since I met her, I let myself believe that we can have a happy life.

# FINALLY

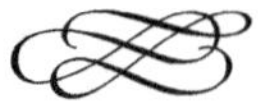

## *LENA*

I can't believe I'm finally back. And I'm not just back in my own time—Mark is with me.

We ended up in a room at the Cable Street Inn. It's beautiful but a bit rundown. The high ceilings, faded wallpaper, and claw-foot tub remind me of the time period I just left. I'd walked past it a dozen times back in 1888 but never once thought I'd be inside. I definitely never thought I'd be lying in one of its beds, trying to convince myself the guy next to me isn't about to disappear.

My mom is probably losing her mind by now, and I should call her soon, but not until we catch our breath. I just need a moment to make sure this is real. I let myself stay like this, pressed against him, listening to the rise and fall of his chest, letting the chaos of the last few weeks settle for a second.

Mark lifts his head off the pillow and looks at me. "How do you think on your feet so quickly like that? The story you told the clerk about the riverboat act... how did you think of that?"

"I don't know, but it worked, didn't it?" I shrug.

He laughs. "Yes, same as when we met. You said you dressed like a man so one wouldn't attack you. You make things up so fast, I barely have time to realize you're lying."

I roll onto my side to face him. "I've studied criminal behavior for years. Once you know how people think, it's not hard to feed them what they need in order to believe your story."

"Well, it's not always a bad thing." His fingers brush my cheek.

"I'm not ashamed of it," I say. "It's not like I'd lie to hurt someone."

He smiles. "I know. We have that in common."

He leans in, and I meet him halfway. The kiss starts slow, and then it deepens. His hand slides into my hair, and I grip the back of his neck. For a second, I stop thinking entirely. No blood, no crime, no impossible timelines. Just the two of us.

Mark pulls me closer. I slide my hands over his shoulders, down his arms and around to his back. His biceps are muscular, his back broad and strong, chiseled with pure muscle.

He kisses down my throat and nibbles my collarbone, his fingertips sliding up and down my thighs. I part my legs and invite him closer. He takes the invitation, untying my robe and discarding it while his mouth finds my breast. I reach down and stroke him until he moans and presses against me harder. I shiver as the bedsprings protest under us. I don't care.

I climb on top of him and ease myself down onto him. He closes his eyes in sheer ecstasy and reaches behind me to squeeze my bottom. I lean forward and grind against him with passionate intensity. It feels like I'm trying to outrun the fear I've felt for months and fall into Mark completely.

He opens his eyes and looks up at me. "You feel amazing," he says. "I don't know how much longer I can last."

That's all I need to push me over the edge. It feels incredible as he fills me, and I lose myself completely.

I pull back and lie still for a moment, letting my body calm down. My head feels clearer now.

After about an hour, I roll onto my side and spot the phone on the nightstand, a beige, plastic landline with a twisted cord. It's a good thing I remember my mom's phone number. It's the only one I know by heart.

When she answers, she sounds breathless. "Hello?"

"Mom?"

There's a pause, one long second, and then, "Oh, my God. Lena?" Her voice cracks. "Where are you? We thought—oh, honey, we thought you were in the river—"

"I know," I say, my throat tightening. "I'm okay. I'm fine. I swear."

"We had people out looking for you." Her words tumble over one another. "The police, search teams... your cousins saw you fall in. They just called off the search for the night at dusk. I thought I'd lost you forever...."

She sobs into the phone.

"Please don't cry, Mom. I'm safe."

There's another pause, and I can hear her quietly crying, trying to get it under control. "Where are you?"

"At the Cable St. Inn," I say. "Are you in London?"

"Of course I am. I came as soon as they told me you were gone. Where's the hotel?"

"Downtown. Room 214, and Mom, could you please bring me some stuff? I need a change of clothes, my wallet, my phone, and some of Tom's clothes, too?"

She hesitates. "Tom's?"

"Yes, please," I say. "I'll explain when you get here."

"Okay," she says finally. "I'll get there as fast as I can."

When I hang up, I turn to Mark. "She's coming," I tell him. "We need to get dressed."

He looks down at the heap of clothes on the floor, our filthy, damp, nineteenth-century clothes.

I pull on my dress, and the fabric's stiff with river water and dirt. It sticks to my skin, cold and rough, but it's better than the pair of us only wearing robes when my mom walks in.

Mark struggles with his pants. "Your mother's going to think we're insane."

"She might," I admit. "But she's going to be too relieved to care."

By the time there's a knock at the door, my heart's racing again. I open it, and my mom is there. I immediately pull her into a hug.

"Oh, my God, Lena," she whispers. "I thought you drowned."

"I'm okay," I assure her.

When she finally pulls away, she notices Mark. Her eyebrows lift, but she doesn't ask. She just sets the bag of clothes on the bed.

"I brought your clothes, phone, wallet, and some of Tom's things."

"Thank you," I say. "Mom," I begin, taking a deep breath. "There's someone I need you to meet, but first we need to change out of these wet clothes."

Mark steps into the bathroom and comes out a minute later wearing Tom's clothes. He looks incredibly hot, sharp, and put-together, like he belongs in this century as much as anyone. I can't stop looking at him. But it's clear he's also slightly uncomfortable in the strange fabrics and cuts.

I go in next and pull on jeans, a T-shirt, and sneakers. After weeks of stiff Victorian fabrics, the soft textures feel different, yet so good—comfortable and familiar.

When I come back out of the bathroom, my mom is sitting in one of the chairs by the window. "I'm glad you're sitting down," I say. "I need to tell you what happened. I didn't just fall into the river. I went back in time–to 1888."

Mom raises her eyebrows, but she doesn't interrupt. I keep going. "That's where we met." I motion to Mark. "His name is Mark Harrow, and he's an inspector. He's one of the lead detectives on the Jack the Ripper case."

I look at Mark. "This is my mom, Meg."

He steps forward. "I know this sounds impossible, but it's true."

She looks between us, disbelief in her eyes. "You… you met him in the 1800s?"

"Yes," I say. "I know it's impossible to believe, but it really happened. Here, only a day has passed, but in 1888… I was there for weeks."

Mom exhales, tilting her head. "Okay… I don't know how to process that. I think you may have just hit your head or are suffering from PTSD from nearly drowning. But you're alive, and that's all that matters."

"I didn't hit my head, Mom. I'm telling you the truth. I can even prove it. Just hear me out."

She studies me for a moment and then nods slowly. "All right. Tell me everything from the start."

I settle into the chair across from her and start at the beginning: how I ended up in Whitechapel, what I saw, what I did, how I met Mark, how we worked together, and the women who died.

Mark fills in gaps, adds things I forget, and he answers her questions when she asks. Mom listens, quiet but focused. She just takes it in.

When I finish, I lean back. "That's it. All of it."

She reaches over and squeezes my hand. "How can you prove this to me, Lena?"

"Do you remember the first five women who died at the hand of the Ripper? We took the tour, and you watched the documentary with me before we left to go on our trip to London."

"Yes. There was Polly, Lizzie, Annie, Catherine, and Mary Jane."

"Exactly," I say, proud that my mother has a memory just like mine. We never forget a name.

"Initially, those were the only five on the list," I say, my voice breaking. Tears spill down my face, and I can't stop myself. "But because of me... Shannon Connor died, too."

Mark pulls me into a hug, holding me tight. "Lena, it's not your fault. None of this is because of you. You did everything you could." Even though his world has been completely upended, he's still so attentive to me.

Mom grabs her phone, her fingers trembling. She scrolls quickly, squinting at the screen. "I... I don't understand. You're saying Shannon didn't initially die?"

It's clear that history has changed because of me. I was hoping maybe it hadn't, but just that one change in one life has altered time.

I pull back enough to meet her eyes. "It was my fault. I was the catalyst. Everything I did... going back in time, me being there, changed things. And now Shannon's dead." I tell her all the details of how Shannon died as Mom looks at her phone, nodding along. She believes me based on the details.

Mark squeezes my shoulders gently. "We're here now. You're back, safe, and you did what you could."

I bury my face in his chest again, letting him hold me. "I just wanted to protect her. I didn't mean for it to happen."

Mom looks from the screen to me. "I believe you, Lena. Not because any of it makes sense but because you're my daughter. You wouldn't lie to me. I don't fully understand, but I believe you."

I take a ragged breath. "Thank you. That's all I needed."

Before I leave the room, I pin Polly's brooch carefully to my shirt. We leave our damp clothing in the trash. When we go down to check out, the clerk trades us the pocket watch for cash. Mark slides his grandfather's pocket watch back into his pocket.

The three of us step onto Cable Street, and I feel dizzy with relief.

Mom hails a cab, and we squeeze in.

"Are we telling anyone else about me?" Mark asks.

I glance at him and then at Mom. "No, not yet. Not everyone needs to know. Just us."

Mom nods. "Agreed."

I lean back, exhaling. "We'll just say you rescued me from the river. That's true. Nothing else. That's the story everyone else gets."

The cab pulls up outside my aunt and uncle's house. We made it. I'm alive, and Mark is here with me.

Mom knocks, and the door swings open before she can finish. Aunt Claire's face lights up when she sees me. "Lena! Oh, thank God. Your mom said she was going to pick you up, but I didn't believe it." She sweeps me into a hug. "Come in, everyone."

I step inside, Mark and Mom right behind me, and the comforting familiarity of the house hits me. The smell of spaghetti sauce fills the air, and my stomach reminds me I haven't eaten in centuries.

As we reach the living room, Uncle Dave, Tom, and Ella are there. Their eyes fill with joyful curiosity when they see me. "Lena?" Tom blurts out, his voice tight. "We thought you drowned!"

I swallow hard, nodding. "I'm fine. Really."

"But we saw you go under," Ella adds. "I cried all night...." Her voice falters.

"It's okay. I'm here now."

Then everyone's eyes fall on Mark. I straighten, clearing my throat. "This is Mark Harrow," I say. "He saved me from the river."

Mark nods politely. "Good to meet you all," he says.

Tom looks bewildered, so I step in before it gets awkward. "His clothes were soaked," I explain quickly. "That's why he's wearing some of yours, Tom."

Tom laughs, shaking his head. "Of course. Only you, Lena."

Ella smiles, relief clear on her face. "We're just glad you're okay."

I glance at Mark, and he gives me the tiniest nod. Our secret is safe.

"Dinner is ready," Aunt Claire declares. "It'll be so nice to have you at the table–both of you."

The meal is full of lots of questions about where I've been. Eventually, after I create a vague story about Mark rescuing me, the topics shift. We talk about the mundane, and the tension in my chest eases with every laugh and every smile. Mark fits in surprisingly well. He answers questions politely, makes a joke or two, and no one presses beyond the river story.

Still, the heaviness of all we've been through doesn't completely fade, and I think it will take some time for me to get used to being back here.

And then I think of Shannon, and it's all I can do to keep tears from filling my eyes.

Wiping his mouth on his napkin, Tom shakes his head. "I still can't believe it. We thought we'd lost you. We had to call a search and rescue party."

"I know," I say apologetically. "I'm sorry all of those people had to go to so much trouble, but I hope they're relieved I'm okay."

After dessert, I push back my chair. "Thank you all for dinner," I say, my voice sincere. "And thank you for searching for me. I'm so glad to be back. But Mark and I are going out. He wants to show me London before I have to go home to New York. We'll be out late, I'm sure. There's no need to wait up." It seems odd to use my phone to call a rideshare, but I'm happy for the convenience.

Mom raises an eyebrow. "Aren't you tired, honey?"

"I'm fine," I lie. The truth is, I'm exhausted, but it's clear Mark needs some time away from my family to get used to this century.

"Just be careful," Mom warns. "You'll be fine, right? You'll stay away from the river?"

"I will," I say. She follows us outside. I take a deep breath of the cool autumn air.

"I'm just going to get Mark a hotel room, and I'll probably stay the night with him there. We are in love, Mom," I say, hugging her.

"As strange as it all is, I'm really happy for you. Text me when you get to the hotel?" Mom says.

"Of course. I love you, Mom. I'll see you tomorrow."

"I love you too, honey."

I slide into the waiting car beside Mark, and for the first time since we met, we don't have to look over our shoulders. We're finally safe.

# A FACE IN THE CROWD

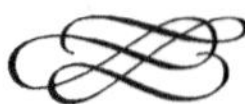

## *LENA*

I WAKE to the buzz of traffic outside and the rhythm of Mark's breathing beside me. It's strange having him here. There's no gas lamps or cobblestone streets echoing with carriage wheels, just sunlight and a city that has traded horses' hooves for car horns.

Mark stirs. "Good morning," he says, his voice rough with sleep. "We are still in London, right?"

"Yes, we're still in London." I playfully toss a pillow at him.

He laughs quietly, running a hand through his hair. "I'll never get used to all this noise."

"It is louder now that I've been away from it for so long. We've got three whole days to see London in this century before I have to start work in New York."

He looks at me, brows raised. "You start your new job in three days?"

"I start Monday morning."

He nods. "Then we should explore. I'd like to see what became of the places I used to walk past every day."

"You're going to be in for a shock," I tease.

He chuckles, shaking his head. "What else is new?"

I grab my phone from the nightstand and call my mom. I tell her

I'm going to take Mark clothes shopping and that we'll meet her at the River Cafe for lunch.

We leave the hotel after breakfast, and the first thing we do is head for Oxford Street. Mark keeps glancing at the traffic like it's a battlefield.

"Does everyone drive like this?" he mutters as a red double-decker bus swerves past.

"Pretty much," I say, laughing. "It's called rush hour. You should see it when it rains."

He shakes his head. "Incredible. All this rushing, despite these vehicles going so much faster than horses."

We duck into a department store, and Mark pauses just inside the entrance, staring up at the escalator.

"They're moving stairs," I explain. "You stand on them, and they take you up."

He looks skeptical. "It doesn't look safe."

I grin. "Neither did time travel, but you managed that."

He gives me a sideways glance but follows me on. The look on his face as we step onto the escalator is priceless: half awe, half suspicion.

Clothing shopping with a man who's used to wool suits and trousers is a challenge. I steer him toward the men's section, handing him jeans, T-shirts, a button-down shirt, and a leather jacket.

He disappears into the fitting room. When he comes out, he looks like he's stepped off the cover of a magazine.

"Well?" he asks, uncertain.

"Dangerously good," I say. "Like, women are going to chase you good."

He smiles. "Then, I'll keep you close so you can protect me from them."

By the time we pay and leave, I've added sunglasses to the pile, just because I want to see him try them. Outside, he puts them on, tilts his head, and frowns.

"These make everything way too dark."

"They're supposed to. That's the point."

He lowers them and gives me a look. "You people have thought of everything."

"Tell me about it." I link my arm through his as we walk toward The Tube.

The River Café sits right on the Thames. Blue-and-white awnings ripple in the breeze as the river glitters just beyond the terrace. Inside, it's open and modern with bright art, vases of fresh flowers, and the scent of basil and olive oil. It's the kind of place where every table seems to shine.

Mom's already seated by the window. She stands when she sees us. "There you are! Oh, Lena, you look rested." Then she turns to Mark. "And how are you this morning, Mr. Harrow?"

He takes her hand, polite as ever. "Please, call me Mark. I'm well, albeit a bit overwhelmed. Thank you. How are you?"

Mom smiles. "I'm wonderful now that my Lena is here—safe. And isn't this such a lovely restaurant?"

"I chose it before we left for London," I explain. "I've always wanted to go mudlarking and eat here. I've certainly done one of those things now."

"Yes," my mother says with a sigh. "And let's not make that mistake again."

The waiter brings glasses of water and a basket of warm bread.

Mom looks at Mark. "So, what do you think of London these days?"

He glances out the window at the river. "It's much louder, and no one seems to look up when they walk. They all have those... phones held up to their faces."

"Ah, yes," she nods. "Everyone's addicted to their devices."

"I noticed," he says dryly. "Half of them would've been robbed blind in Whitechapel in my day."

Mom laughs. "I like him. He's funny."

I can't help but grin. "I like him, too."

We eat grilled fish with lemon and a cucumber and tomato salad that tastes like summer. For dessert, we have chocolate cake so rich it almost feels indecent.

When Mom excuses herself to take a call, Mark leans closer. "Is this what you imagined?"

"Not even close," I whisper. "It's so much better."

We step out of the River Café, and I notice the air smells so much cleaner than it did in the nineteenth century, which is surprising. The smog created by all that coal burning was even worse than what the cars put out.

Mom stands close to me as we wait for a cab, talking about how good it felt to have a proper meal that no one in our family had to cook.

"That chocolate cake," she sighs. "I think I'm still in love with it."

"You and me both," I say, smiling.

Mark stands a few steps away, watching everything with fascination. There's something childlike in the way he studies the cars, buses, and people. He's seeing a world rebuilt on top of his own.

A cab pulls up, and Mom gets in first, then I slide in. "We're going to Aunt Claire's?" she asks.

"Yes," I nod. "I want to make sure I spend plenty of time with the family while I'm here."

Mark climbs in last, and Mom gives the address to the cabbie, who merges into traffic.

I turn toward the window, absently watching people cross the bridge, and then I freeze.

Across the street, standing near the river's edge, is a man in a dark coat, his hat pulled low. He's tall, still, and oddly out of place in the motion of the city. He stares directly at me, and when the sunlight hits his face, my stomach flips.

He looks exactly like Kosminski.

It's his posture and his eyes.

But… didn't he die in the river?

When a red bus roars past, it blocks my view. Then it passes, and he's gone.

"Lena?" Mom's voice cuts through. "Are you all right?"

"Yeah," I say too quickly. "Just thought I saw someone I knew."

She nods, distracted, pulling her phone from her bag.

I keep my gaze fixed out the window, scanning the crowd. Nothing, just strangers. Maybe I imagined it. Maybe my mind is playing tricks on me.

When we get to Aunt Claire's house, she opens the door, beaming. "Lena! I'm glad you came back to see us before you have to leave."

"I couldn't stay away," I say, smiling as she hugs me.

"Mark, it's good to see you again. Are you sure you can survive another evening with us?" she jokes.

"Dinner last night was a pleasure," he says politely as we all step inside the kitchen.

Uncle Dave looks out from behind the pantry door. "We were about to pour a glass of wine. Would anyone like one?"

"I'd like two." Mom laughs, setting her bag down. "We're celebrating Lena tonight."

Aunt Claire sits on a barstool at the counter. "How are you feeling about your new job, Lena?"

I manage a grin, letting my fear from before fade away. I probably just imagined it. I've been so scared of the Ripper for so long. "I'm very excited and *very* nervous."

Uncle Dave raises an eyebrow. "It'll be intense, but you'll be amazing at it."

"It's not anything I haven't already experienced," I say. "Uh... in class, I mean."

Uncle Dave pours five glasses of red wine, one for each of us. "To Lena and her new job," he says, lifting his glass.

"To Lena and her new job," they echo, clinking glasses gently together.

Aunt Claire leans on the counter. "So, Mark, tell us what is it that you do for a living?"

"I'm a detective," Mark says.

"Oh!" Aunt Claire's eyebrows rise. "Well, that is certainly interesting."

Uncle Dave smiles. "You two are a good match then. A criminal profiler and a detective. That's perfect."

Mom laughs. "It really is. Good thing the two of you met." She winks at me.

The kitchen door opens, and Ella steps in. "I thought I'd come see what all the commotion was about."

"Perfect timing." Aunt Claire smiles. "We were just catching up and celebrating your cousin's new job."

Ella hops onto a stool at the counter. "Well, I'll happily join the celebration."

Aunt Claire gets another glass. "It's a shame Tom couldn't be here tonight. He's at work, but I'm sure he would have enjoyed this as much as the rest of us."

I nod. "We'll fill him in later."

We sit together, talking and laughing, the hours slipping by easily. It feels good to be back, surrounded by my family. I realize how much I've missed being here, in my own time, with people who matter. I don't allow myself to think about Shannon or the Ripper. It's the only way to keep my mind at ease.

When it's finally time to leave, I hug everyone tightly, promising to see them again soon. Mark stands beside me, and together we head back to the hotel. The cab ride is calm, neither of us saying much, just holding onto the simple contentment of the day.

Back in the hotel, I buy a notebook and a pack of pens from the gift shop, and we head up to the room.

Mark drops onto the bed, leaning back with a hand over his eyes. "Today was… interesting," he murmurs. "The city. The culture shock. Your family. All of it."

"Yeah," I say. "I'm sure you're exhausted."

I glance out the window and feel anxiety creep in. Did I really see Kosminski earlier? Telling myself it couldn't have been. I shake my head, forcing the thought down. I don't want to tell Mark yet, not until I know I'm not just being paranoid.

"Okay," I say, sitting down at the table with my notebook. "We need to figure out how to get you on the flight. Paperwork, ID, tickets… everything has to be ready."

Mark sits up, rubbing the back of his neck. "It sounds complicated."

I swallow and nod. "It will be, but we can manage it—though not legally. Thankfully, I have some contacts from school. I need to make a list." I pull out a pen and start ticking items, and every box I draw makes my heart race a little faster. There's no margin for error, and we only have two days.

Mark watches me. "You seem tense, Lena."

"I'm fine," I lie, smiling at him.

I'm not fine, not really. I keep thinking about that man by the river, the way he stood there, staring. But I push it down. I can't think about that now. We have to make a plan. We have to focus.

Mark reaches over and takes my hand. "Hey, we'll figure it out together, just like we always do."

Step by step, task by task, we'll get Mark on that plane. I'll start my new job, and everything will work out fine.

I finish the list, close my notebook, and stretch back on the bed, letting the tension ease. Tomorrow, we'll tackle the next part. Tonight, I allow myself this—a few hours of rest, and just being with Mark, trying to hold the pieces of my life together, even as the dangers of 1888 linger at the edges of my thoughts.

# FREE TO KILL

## *MARK*

Iᴛ's our last full day in London, and we both rise and dress early. Once we're ready, Lena pulls what she calls her laptop toward her and places the phone to her ear. I head down to the lobby to grab some breakfast for both of us.

When I return, she's still talking on her phone, her tone professional and businesslike. "Detective Lena Carter, NYPD. Badge 4782, employee number 274-09-12. I'm calling from London on official business. We need a virtual witness protection packet applied to the system. We are in London with the witness. The tangible documents will need to be waiting at JFK on arrival. Name to be registered: Mark Harrow."

She listens to a list of requirements and rattles off confirmations. "Yes, I can provide ID numbers, case reference, and an authorization code. I'll be sending over an affidavit and a signed request."

She finishes the phone call, and I set coffee, a breakfast sandwich, and a bottle of water next to her on the table. She shoots me a grateful smile. "You're spoiling me," she murmurs.

"Grabbing breakfast is much easier than trying to wrap my head around the logistics of what you're doing or any of the words you're using."

She laughs, finishes typing on the device, and looks up at me, beaming. "There," she says. "They'll fast-track the virtual packet, and the physical documents will be at the arrivals office. Name change recorded as Mark Harrow. Flight confirmation is attached. We should still expect security checks, but the problem is contained. It might not be completely legal or ethical, but it will work. The virtual packet includes photo match overrides. As long as you hand them the papers and don't panic, the system will accept you."

"I can't believe you did all that for me." I shake my head and smile. "And somehow you made it look simple."

She leans into me, tired and triumphant. "I'm just glad my employee and badge numbers were already in the system. We'll still have to be careful," she says. "But it's a start."

I pull her close and whisper, "I love you."

She kisses my cheek and answers without missing a beat. "I love you, too."

When we finish breakfast, Lena checks the time. "Before we leave tomorrow, I want to try something."

Her tone tells me we are about to have another Lena style adventure. "What sort of something?"

"The Metropolitan Police Museum," she says. "They've got an archive room with records from the 1800s. I want to see how the Ripper case changed since I interfered in time and we both disappeared."

It takes only a short cab ride to get there, and I quietly wonder if I'll ever grow accustomed to this. Once inside the museum, a clerk leads us through a security door into the record room.

The place smells like old paper and dust. Shelves stretch from floor to ceiling, lined with boxes marked *MEPO* with dates and numbers scrawled on their sides. The clerk gestures to a table. "You can request up to three boxes at a time. Please handle the contents carefully and wear gloves."

Lena fills out the slip. I watch her neat handwriting, steady and certain. *Case files, Whitechapel murders, 1888–1889.*

When the boxes arrive, the weight of them hits me like a ghost.

They look harmless, just gray cardboard, but inside are the years I lived through, the men I knew, and the women who died. Some of them even have my handwriting on them.

We open the first box filled with letters, statements, and police orders. Lena lifts one sheet, and I see familiar names written in ink faded to brown: *Inspector Abberline. Inspector Harrow. Corporal Finch. Constable Parker. Constable Clarke.*

"Here," she says, pulling a small leather journal from the bundle. The leather is cracked, the initials *R.P.* faintly visible. "Is the RP for Roger Parker?" she asks, setting the journal between us and flipping it open.

I nod and hold my breath.

The first pages are routine: dates, charges, arrests, nothing unusual. Then Lena gasps. Her eyes move faster across the lines. "Mark," she whispers. "Listen to this."

She reads aloud. "*Another one tonight. The streets were thick with filthy women, as usual. Clarke says the birds bring it on themselves, flaunting sin where decent folk have to walk. I can't say I disagree. If the whores were gone, the city might breathe easier. The Ripper's doing what all of us want to do. There's justice in it.*"

I stare at the page. The handwriting is undoubtedly Parker's. Instantly, I'm filled with rage.

Lena turns another page. "*Clarke and I followed her down Hanbury Street and didn't stop her. The Ripper was lurking in the shadows of her house. We knew it, and we let it happen. Better the boss think we're fools than have them know we stood aside.*"

Lena's hands tremble slightly. "They *let* him kill her. There's more. '*We sent another to the papers today. Clarke thought of the heading 'Dear Boss.' It will keep them chasing. Let the Ripper have his fun. London will thank us in time when all the whores are gone.*'

I can barely breathe. The words blur. "They weren't *just* turning a blind eye," I say. "They were helping him."

Lena nods, her eyes filled with sadness. "Parker and Clarke wrote some of the *Dear Boss* letters. They let women be followed and murdered, and they sabotaged the investigation."

"They hated those women," I mutter. "Thought killing them cleaned the streets." I remember when Parker and Clarke had us chasing the wrong suspect, which eventually got Shannon killed and me fired. "We thought maybe one of them was the Ripper himself. Turns out, they just wanted him free to kill more women."

Lena closes the notebook gently. "This explains a lot."

"That explains our suspicions of those two bloody bastards, that's for damn certain."

It is reassuring to see that the murders stopped after Shannon, although there was suspicion that the Ripper may have murdered both Lena and me. It was odd to see my name in a report like that–noted as missing, body never recovered.

My poor mother. But I can't think about that now because there's absolutely nothing I can do about it.

We leave the museum just before dusk, and Lena threads her arm through mine as we walk back to the street, our hearts heavy with what we just read. Neither of us can shake the ugliness buried in those files, the truth that men I once called colleagues helped the Ripper.

By the time we reach the restaurant where we're meeting everyone, we've both forced smiles back onto our faces. Lena's mum Meg waves from the window, beckoning us inside where the rest of Lena's family is already gathered. Her Aunt Claire and Uncle Dave stand to hug her, and Tom and Ella are there, too.

Tonight, we're dining at Dishoom Covent Garden, which is very exotic, the smell of cardamom wafting from the kitchen.

"You two made it just in time. We ordered samosas and paneer to start," Meg says.

Lena smiles. "You guys always pick the best places."

We talk about flights, plans, and New York. Tom tells a story about nearly missing his train because of a street magician. I try to take it all in, but I can't help thinking about how impossible it is that I'm sitting here, a century and a half from where I started, surrounded by Lena's family, eating spiced lentils and naan bread instead of boiled potatoes.

Then, across the room, I see a man at the bar. His narrow facial features, dark wavy hair combed to the side, and dark eyes that seem to look through me make my heart lurch. For a split second, I swear it's Kosminski. A waiter walks between us, and I crane my neck to see him, but then he's gone.

Lena nudges me, whispering, "Are you okay?"

"Yes," I lie. "I'm fine. Just checking out the wine selection."

She squeezes my knee under the table, and I make myself smile again, though my pulse doesn't slow down.

Dinner stretches late. There's dessert, wine, goodbyes at the door, and promises to visit again soon. Meg hugs us both hard before we step into the night air.

Back at the hotel, we pack our bags. Exhausted, we climb into bed. In the dark, Lena curls against me.

I lie awake a while longer, staring at the ceiling, thinking about those files, about Parker and Clarke, and about the man I saw at the bar.

It was just my imagination. It has to be.

I WAKE TO THE SOUND OF LENA MOVING AROUND. SHE'S ALREADY dressed, her hair tied up, phone in hand. I dress quickly, and we pack the last of our things and head down to the front desk. Lena speaks with the clerk briefly and then taps a few buttons on her phone. Moments later, she hands me a small stack of papers.

"We're all set," she says. "It's everything you need to get on the plane and into America."

I stare at her in awe. "You really do think of everything."

We get into a cab and ride through streets I barely notice. At her aunt's house, Lena dashes inside for one last round of goodbyes. I bid them all farewell, and then it's time for me to leave London.

Meg climbs into the car beside me, cheerful and reassuring. "You'll love New York," she says.

We head to the airport, and I have no idea what to expect a plane ride to be like, despite Lena's prior reassurances.

When the airport comes into view, my whole body tightens with nervous energy. Lena notices and takes my hand. "It's okay," she whispers.

Meg nods. "You'll be fine once we get on the plane."

The airplanes flying overhead seem impossibly large, and I can't stop staring. "I thought buses were huge and intimidating…."

Inside, Lena moves through the lines confidently. She hands over papers, answers questions with authority, and somehow keeps calm and orderly. I follow her, clutching the documents she's given me, still trying to process how she made all of this work.

We pass through security without trouble. The crowd closes in from all sides, voices blending into a roar. Then I notice a man in a dark coat, his hat pulled low. He looks like Kosminski, but then he's gone, swallowed by the crowd. I tell myself it's impossible, that he died in the river. Even if he somehow survived, he'd have no way of getting the documents he'd need to follow us—would he? It's just my mind conjuring up ghosts from another life.

I force my attention back to Lena, who's talking and laughing with her mum. The sound of their voices comforts me, but I can't shake the feeling that someone is watching us.

Finally, we reach the gate, and my stomach clenches at the thought of stepping onto an airplane. Lena squeezes my hand again. "It's really safe," she says. "You'll see. There's nothing to worry about."

I nod, trying to take deep breaths. While we wait, I watch other planes take off, one after another. It's frightening, yes, but somehow, it's exhilarating, too.

They call our group number, and we move toward the entrance of the plane. Another glance behind us, and I swear I see that dark coat and old-fashioned hat one last time, disappearing into the crowd. If he can manage to get into the airport, he should be able to find new clothes, right? I shake it off, focusing on the metal bird waiting to carry me into a new life.

We step onto the plane together. Lena helps me find my seat and buckles me in tight. I'm seated between her and her mother, which makes me feel a little more assured. Lena whispers in my ear while the plane is preparing, and when it takes off, she holds my hand. It's not as frightening as I imagined. In fact, it's kind of fun. Seeing the city from this height, flying through the clouds, it's like a dream—something I never thought would be possible.

Hours later, the plane lands with a jolt. The airport is just as loud as the one we left from. I try to block it all out and follow Lena through the lines. We have no problem making it into the country.

Outside, New York City expands all around me. Towers claw at the sky, streets are crammed with cars, and the people move like insects, scattering everywhere all at once. It's loud, chaotic, and yet, somehow, it feels alive in a way I recognize. "This place reminds me of Whitechapel," I murmur.

"I can see that. Dirty, loud, crazy, and dangerous." Lena laughs.

The cab ride through the city is a blur of color and movement. I try to take in every detail. The smells, the sounds, the fast-paced inertia of the streets—it's all kind of beautiful. As I try to absorb it, my thoughts keep drifting.

Was that Kosminski I saw at the airport in London? And worse, did he follow us across the Atlantic?

It's a paranoid thought, yet it keeps clawing at the back of my mind.

What if we're not safe after all?

# NOT JUST A WALK IN THE PARK

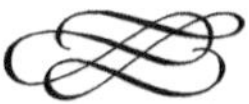

## *LENA*

THE CITY MOVES FAST, and since I returned, I've had to move even faster. Two weeks back in New York, and I'm already elbow-deep in case files, interviews, and forensic reports. My first day as the NYPD's newest forensic psychologist was a blur of handshakes and passwords. The day I started, I spent a long night deleting every trace of the witness protection request I'd filed in London, with the help of some friends overseas who owed me some favors. It's gone now, erased from every database that could have gotten me fired before I even got my official badge. I'm still working on getting Mark the paperwork he needs, which will be even more illegal than getting him to New York, but he's worth it.

In the mornings, Mark kisses me goodbye before I leave for work. He's still in awe of the twenty-first century, and I can't blame him. It's so very different from the Victorian era he's used to. I got him a phone last week, and although he usually forgets to charge it overnight, he calls me every afternoon while I'm on lunch, proud of some new discovery. He loves the corner café that makes the best coffee, a park bench with a view of the river, and a bookstore where no one looks twice if he spends hours reading.

When I get home, the apartment smells like whatever he's tried to cook. Some nights it's edible, but most nights, we end up ordering delivery. Honestly, I'm just happy to have him here with me, even when the apartment smells like burned fish.

Mark's been restless lately, though. He has too strong a work ethic and sense of pride to just wander the city forever. Last night over dinner, I told him he should consider becoming a private investigator. He laughed at first, thinking I was joking, but the truth is, he's perfect for it. He's seen the worst of humanity and still believes in justice. He notices details most detectives miss.

We've fallen into a rhythm. We have coffee together in the morning; he kisses me goodbye at the door, and I call him when my shift runs late. He's learning to navigate this century: the noise, the pace, the "strange magic," as he calls it. Sometimes I catch him looking at the skyline from the window, his eyes distant, and I wonder if he misses London, his mother, and the life he left behind.

Each night, he pulls me close and whispers something romantic as his hands roam over me, and I melt into him. His lips follow every curve of my body, sending sparks through me.

He makes the past feel far away. And while the future is uncertain, it's ours to write together. When I wake in the dark and feel his arm around me, I know that somehow, through time, chaos, and everything that should have torn us apart, we're building something solid—together.

ON MY FIRST *REAL* LUNCH BREAK IN WEEKS, MOM INSISTS ON MEETING me near Bryant Park. She's been over the moon since we came home from London. She's always checking on me like I'm going to vanish again.

I let her choose the place today. It's a little French café with outdoor tables and bright yellow umbrellas. She's already there when I arrive, sitting at the table with two iced teas and a big smile. We catch up on everything from her yoga class to her neighbor's new dog and a documentary she swears I'll love. It feels good. It feels normal–until I glance across the street.

There's a man on the opposite curb, standing too still for too long. He's wearing a long dark coat, and his face is shadowed by the brim of a hat. Even though it's a modern day hat, not that top hat from the 1800s, I know for certain this time that it's Kosminski.

My fork shakes in my hand. Suddenly, I'm back where the fog is thick, the street is slick with rain, and Shannon's lying on the ground in a pool of blood.

"Lena?" Mom's voice cuts through. I jerk my head and try to focus on her face. "Are you okay, sweetheart?"

"Yeah," I lie. "I just zoned out."

I look again, and he's gone. The space where he stood is filled with other passersby. I force a smile, but my heartbeat won't slow down.

The rest of lunch passes in fragments I barely catch. I pay the bill before Mom can argue and insist on riding in the cab with her back to her building. The whole time, I keep checking behind us. I don't see him, but that doesn't soothe me.

When we get to her first-floor apartment, I unlock the door for her and enter first. I tell her I need to use her bathroom, but it's just an excuse to check every nook and cranny of her apartment before I leave. I can't bear the thought of letting what happened to Mary Jane happen to my own mother. The idea sends a chill down my spine.

I head back to the office, but finishing my work is difficult. All I can think about is him. How did he get here? And what is he going to do next?

After work, I grab a cab home. Mark's sitting by the window, reading one of the crime novels he's been devouring lately. He looks up as soon as I walk in. "You look like you've seen a ghost." He closes the book and sets it aside.

"I think I may have."

He stands, concern immediately replacing the light in his eyes. "What happened?"

I drop my bag onto the couch and sit, trying to calm myself. "Kosminski. I saw him today. The way he watched us, Mark, I know it was him."

He stares at me for a long moment, the color draining from his face. "You're certain?"

I nod. "I wish I weren't."

With a deep breath, he holds me tight. "It's 2025, and we're in New York. This is different. If it's him, it'll be a lot more difficult for him to kill anyone."

I nod into his shoulder, but we both know that's not true. Murders happen by the dozens every day in this city. They might not follow his M.O., but he can adapt. We both know that.

The next few days, I keep my eyes open and a weapon on me at all times, but with Mark's reassurance, I begin to feel like maybe it was just my imagination.

"It's just your mind playing tricks," he says one evening. He pulls me onto the couch, lets me lean against him, and I close my eyes, trying to convince myself that he's right, that Kosminski is dead.

A few nights later, we go on a dinner date at a little Italian place near Washington Square. The food is delicious, the wine is even better, and we're having an incredible time.

After dinner, we leave the restaurant and walk down the street, holding hands.

That's when I catch him out of the corner of my eye, standing across the street. My heart races as panic washes over me. I turn to look right at him, and I know for a fact it's him. I've seen him too many times now to be wrong.

Kosminski.

Mark tenses beside me, his hand gripping mine. He steps in front of me protectively. "Lena—"

"I see him," I whisper.

Kosminski runs and this time, we don't chase him.

"Not tonight, you bastard." Mark's fingers are still tight around mine, both of us staring at the empty stretch of sidewalk where the Ripper stood a second ago.

"Let's go home," I choke out.

Mark doesn't argue. He just nods, his jaw clenched, scanning the corners, the alleys, and the moving cars. We hail a cab, and by the time we reach the apartment, my hands are shaking uncontrollably. Mark locks the door, checks it twice, then drags the chain across. I close every window blind.

Next, I move to my desk and switch on my police scanner, filling the room with the familiar static and coded language of the city.

Mark sinks onto the couch, his elbows on his knees, but I pace. My badge sits on the counter where I dropped it earlier, the NYPD crest catching the lamplight. I should call someone. I should report what I saw. But what would I say? *The man who murdered women in Whitechapel in 1888 just followed me through time?*

I'd be locked in the psych ward before sunrise. So instead, I call a friend from the precinct, Detective Ortiz, and ask him to bring me two Glocks and an unmarked car. He owes me for smoothing a situation over with his boss last week, so even though it's a big ask, he has to come through.

At first, he thinks I'm joking. "Why on earth could you possibly need those?" Ortiz sounds half amused, half suspicious.

"I'll tell you when you get here," I say, keeping my voice light.

As we wait, we continue to listen for signs of the Ripper in New York.

"Unit twelve, domestic on East 74th."

"Possible break-in, 212 West 123rd St."

"Robbery, deli, 2nd Avenue."

Hours pass. Midnight bleeds into 1:00 o'clock, then around 2:00, there's a sharp knock on the door. I look through the eye hole before opening it and see Detective Ortiz and his partner standing in the hallway, their expressions a mix of curiosity and caution.

I open the door. "Detective Ortiz," I say, stepping aside to let them in. "And you must be...."

"Detective Crocket," his partner says, offering a firm handshake. "It's a pleasure to meet you, Dr. Carter."

I nod, motioning them further inside. "I'm glad you could make it. This is my boyfriend, Mark," I add.

"Thank you for helping us out," Mark says.

Ortiz sets two sleek Glocks on the table and then reaches into his coat pocket and takes out a set of car keys.

"And what exactly do you need these for?" he asks, dangling the keys just out of reach.

"A dangerous man with a personal vendetta against me is following me. I need to be ready for anything."

Crocket frowns but doesn't interrupt. Ortiz hands me the keys. "All right. I trust you know what you're doing. The car is parked in the lot in front of your building, black sedan."

I tuck the keys into my pocket. Ortiz glances at the Glocks again and then back to me. "Let's hope you don't have to use those."

"I agree, Detective. Thank you, but I have one more favor to ask. Could I borrow a pair of handcuffs?"

Ortiz shoots me another suspicious look but then pulls the handcuffs from his belt and hands them over. "Don't have too much fun with these." He winks, and I wish I had the energy to laugh at his joke.

After the detectives leave, the scanner crackles again, but it's just more domestic calls, a traffic stop, and a noise complaint.

Then, at 3:04 A.M., a voice comes through. "Central, 911 caller reports a woman down in Central Park. Possible homicide. Throat wound. Units responding."

I sit up straight, staring at the scanner like I might have heard wrong, but the dispatcher repeats it, clearer this time.

"It's him," Mark says. "No question."

I nod, my heart beating out of my chest. He followed us through time. He wanted to kill me, but since he couldn't, he found someone else.

Another innocent woman.

Dead.

Jack the Ripper is here.

# A HUNCH

*MARK*

THE CITY THAT NEVER SLEEPS—THERE couldn't be a more accurate description. Lena sits across from me at the kitchen table among files spread out like a paper battlefield. We scour crime scene photos, the autopsy report, and witness statements. It's almost 1:00 in the morning. I should be exhausted, but the adrenaline keeps me going.

She brings her work home every night now, the same way we used to spread maps and case notes across my coffee table back in my time.

The victim's name was Rita Shaw. She was thirty-four, arrested twice for solicitation, and she was found in Central Park near the reservoir. Her throat was slit, her abdomen mutilated. We know he did it.

Lena pushes another witness statement toward me, and it brings me back to Whitechapel. But this isn't 1888. The lights are brighter now, and the tools are sharper. The police techniques, the DNA labs, the endless databases. It should make catching him easier. Yet, he's still out there—for now.

I pick up the witness statement, reading the neat print. A jogger saw a man near the scene. He describes him as tall, wearing a trench coat with his collar up, and a hat.

Lena leans closer, her eyes scanning my notes. "He's changed his hunting ground, but not his pattern. He'll kill again soon." She closes the folder. "We have to catch him this time."

I want to believe that. I want to believe that the two of us can end what began in London over a century ago. But deep down, I know Kosminski isn't just killing to kill. He's proving that he can do whatever he wants and never get caught. He sees this city as just another playground.

THE NEXT MORNING IS SATURDAY, SO WE SLEEP IN, AND IT'S NEARLY afternoon before we awaken. I start the coffee first and then run down to the lobby to get the mail for Lena. I reach into the slot and pull out the usual bills, flyers, and one envelope that makes my blood boil.

I race back up to the apartment. Lena's still in the shower, and I take the opportunity to look over the letter before she sees it.

My name sits beside hers in neat, slanted handwriting that makes my chest go cold. **Harrow & Carter.**

Inside, there's a single sheet of paper folded once.

*Dear Doc,*

**The bird in the park was a practice stroke before the real art begins again.**

**Meg sure keeps late hours for a woman her age.**

*Sincerely,*

*Jack*

I tighten my fingers around the paper. It's the same phrasing, same rhythm as the letters he sent in Whitechapel. The mocking tone and the performative courtesy, but this time, he's threatening Lena's mum.

Lena steps into the room, towel drying her hair, just as I fold the page. "What's that?"

"It's from him. You need to sit down before you read it."

I hand it to her, watching her expression change as she reads. Her face contorts into fury and fear, but she doesn't look away. When she finally speaks, her voice is calm. "He knows where my mother lives."

She sinks into the chair, the letter trembling in her hands. "We'll stop him before he gets near her. Kosminski doesn't make idle threats. When he writes, someone bleeds."

She texts her mom that we're coming over and not to go outside, and we drive straight to Meg's apartment. Lena's hands are tight on the wheel, and her jaw is locked. Every time she glances in the rearview mirror, I do, too. I see nothing but headlights... but still, I don't relax.

When we reach the apartment building, I scan both sides of the street before we get out. Meg opens the door in her robe, confusion turning to worry when she sees our faces.

"What happened?" she asks.

Lena steps inside first. "You can't stay here tonight."

Her mother looks even more puzzled. "Why? What's going on?"

"The Ripper followed us," Lena explains. "He sent another letter, and this time he mentioned you by name."

Meg gasps. "My God."

"I know it's hard to believe, Mom, but I've seen him with my own eyes. We need to get you someplace safe right away." Lena wraps her arms around her mother and squeezes.

"What about you?" Meg asks. "You're not going to confront him yourself, are you?"

"Of course not," Lena says without missing a beat. She meets my eyes over her mother's head. "I'll contact the police chief and tell him."

She sounds convincing–convincing enough to fool her own mother–but not me.

We wait for Meg to get dressed, and then Lena grabs her mum's coat from the rack, wraps it around her shoulders, and guides her out the door.

We get Meg into a hotel room, and then Lena calls in a favor with her co-worker and friend on the police force, Detective Ortiz. He promises to keep an eye on the hotel, to check the floor regularly, and to make sure no one suspicious comes or goes. He also says he'll talk to the doorman, someone he knows and trusts.

Once we're in the car again, Lena turns to me. "Do you think he'll come tonight?" she asks.

"He might. He's probably champing at the bit to take another life."

We park a block from Meg's apartment building and then make our way down the street, slipping into her apartment through the back door. Inside, we move from room to room, securing windows and doors but leaving the lights on to make it look as though she's home.

Then... we wait.

I'm hopeful that the Ripper will strike that first night, that the confrontation will be over soon, that we'll finally get this over with.

But the night passes without incident, and into the second day, Lena and I start to doubt our decision. What if he followed us? What if he knows where Meg is?

We hunker down, dozing during the day, taking turns watching and listening all night.

The third night, I'm in the bathroom, splashing cold water on my face to try to stay awake when I hear footsteps. My blood runs cold. It's him—it has to be.

My fingers wrap around the gun I laid on the sink, and I rush to the bedroom just in time to hear the shatter of glass. With my heart in my throat, I round the corner just as Lena shrieks.

A hulking shadow looms near the window by the bed. Moonlight glints off the steel blade of a knife held against Lena's throat. Her eyes are wide as she claws at his arm, staring at me.

"You thought you could get away from me, didn't you, little bird?" Kosminski growls. "Even a trip through time can't stop me."

"Let her go," I growl, raising the gun and pointing it at his head.

Kosminski's laugh is low and rumbling like thunder before a storm. "Are you ready to watch her bleed all over the sheets?"

I've fired a gun at him before, but it's not a weapon we used on the force in London, and this one is different than what I'm used to. I've practiced with it a bit since Lena gave it to me a few days ago, but I've never fired it. What if I miss? What if I hit Lena?

"I will kill you," I say, cocking the gun. "Did you come all this way just to die?"

"You can't kill a ghost," Kosminski whispers in a haunting growl.

The blade moves in the dim light, and I know I have to act now, or Lena will die. I take aim, but just before I pull the trigger, Lena slams her knee up, catching him right in the groin. The knife slides against her throat as he howls in pain. She pushes the blade away with one arm and shoves her elbow back into his gut with the other, pushing off him.

I pull the trigger, and Kosminski falls to the ground.

"Lena!" Closing the distance, I lunge for her, and she falls into my arms. On the ground, Kosminski grapples for the knife that's fallen out of his hand. I slam my boot down on his hand, and he cries out again. Lena kicks the blade away, and I move to contain him.

"Bloody hell!" Kosminski screams. "No, you can't stop me. No one can!"

"It's over, Ripper," I tell him, keeping my knee buried in his back while Lena calls the police. I can see her hands trembling as she fumbles with her phone, and a bead of blood trickles down her neck—but she's all right.

Kosminski, on the other hand, is bleeding from the shoulder. Part of me wishes I would've shot him in the head, to make sure he could never hurt anyone again, but at least this way he'll pay for what he did to that poor woman in the park. I twist his arms behind his back, and Lena hands me the handcuffs. The bastard isn't going anywhere.

Minutes drag out, seeming like hours, as I hold Kosminski down, and we wait for the police. Finally, beams of red and blue flood through the broken window. Lena rushes to the door to let them in, and several officers hurry into the apartment.

"Captain Reyes," Lena says. "I'm so glad you're here."

Officers rush over to take over for me as Lena's boss surveys the situation. "Dr. Carter," Reyes says. "Please explain."

"I caught this man breaking in," Lena says, calmly and in control. She steps to the dining room table and picks up a sheet of paper, handing it to him. "I received this letter a few days ago. This is my mother's apartment. He threatened her, so I was waiting for him. I believe his name is Aaron Kosminski. I have reason to believe his

DNA will match the sample from Rita Shaw, the woman who was recently murdered in Central Park."

Reyes nods, and one of the officers hauls Kosminski up to his feet. The officer says in a calm voice, "You have the right to remain silent...." He has no idea he's speaking to Jack the Ripper.

The next several minutes are a whirlwind as police come and go through their procedures. I watch in awe, noting all the changes that have been made over the years. Yellow tape, evidence collection, photographs, it's all so interesting–and a welcomed distraction for me.

We just caught Jack the Ripper....

Captain Reyes claps Lena on the shoulder. "You could've gotten yourself killed, you know? If anything like this ever happens again, let me know before it goes down, huh?"

"I'm sorry, sir. You're right, though I truly hope there won't ever be a next time."

"You've got spunk and moxie, Dr. Carter. I'll give you that," Captain Reyes says.

By the time the cruisers pull away, it's nearly dawn. Lena stands beside me on the curb, her hair falling loose around her shoulders, the reflection of the flashing lights fading from her eyes. Kosminski is finally gone, locked in the back of a police car.

I take a deep breath and wrap Lena in my arms. "It's over," I whisper, kissing the top of her head.

"It's finally over." She smiles up at me, and I feel the weight of a century of worry falling from my shoulders.

Justice will finally be served–not just for Rita but for the others as well. In my mind, I say their names, picture their faces, and pray that they are at peace.

Mary "Polly" Nichols.

Annie Chapman.

Elizabeth Stride.

Catherine Eddowes.

Mary Kelley.

Shannon Connor.

I'll never forget them.

# NO MORE MONSTERS

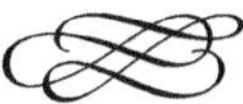

## *LENA*

IT'S BEEN a year since they led Aaron Kosminski out of my mom's apartment in handcuffs, a full year of hearings, testimony, and long days sitting beside Mark in the front row while the monster stood trial.

The early winter air has begun to bite, and evenings come too quickly, casting gloomy shadows across the streets like reminders of everything we'd endured. Standing outside the courtroom on late evenings, I see shadows take shape, forming a man in a top hat with a long coat. I blink them away.

The verdict finally comes. The jury didn't take long to find him guilty on all counts. When the judge reads the sentence, life without parole, Mark squeezes my hand, and I feel it all at once: relief, exhaustion, and triumph.

The hunt that began in the dirty alleys of Whitechapel over a hundred years ago finally ended here, in a New York City courtroom. Kosminski's reign of terror is over. The man who chased us through centuries, who hunted Mark, my mother, and me, will never hurt anyone again.

Now, life feels different, and the papers have finally stopped printing Kosminski's name. For a while, they had a field day comparing him to Jack the Ripper, especially since he shared the name of the main suspect from the infamous case. Headlines screamed, theories flourished, but now even that frenzy has faded, and no one would ever believe that Kosminski and the Ripper really are one and the same.

Mark is adjusting to life in my time. He still feels out of place sometimes, but he's learned how to navigate this century. He started his own agency, *Harrow Investigations,* out of a small brick building on Canal Street. People like him. They don't always know what to make of him, but they respect him.

He still jokingly calls smartphones "witchcraft." But he's mastered texting, email, the subway, and New York pizza, which he insists is "decidedly superior to anything Victorian London ever produced." We are carving out a life here together, and it's been more wonderful than anything I could've predicted.

When I ask if he misses his mother or his own time, he smiles and admits he does, though he knows she was growing older, and their time together would have been limited. It still saddens him that he never got to say goodbye, that she didn't ever know what happened to him, but he holds onto the memory of the life they shared when he was a child, and the last time he saw her... when she met me. He believes she greatly approved of me and would've been happy knowing he has found his own happiness.

Still, sometimes when I wake up and see him making coffee in the kitchen, it hits me again just how impossible all of this is and how lucky I am that he's here with me.

It's a cold winter afternoon when Mark and I exit our apartment building. I sling my bag over my shoulder and meet Mark's eyes. "Ready?" I ask.

"As ready as I'll ever be." We climb into the car we've recently bought together and head out.

There's no more chasing, no more hearings, no more sitting in courtrooms. Today isn't about evidence, ghosts or justice. It's about confronting a monster.

Mark drops me off in front of the prison just after noon and heads to the parking lot to wait. I told my boss this was for work. I said I wanted to conduct a final interview for my ongoing research on criminal pathology, and that isn't a complete lie. My boss signed off on it without much pushback. After all, who better than me to try to understand the mind of Aaron Kosminski?

Inside, the air smells like disinfectant and body odor. The guard leads me through a series of locked doors, each one shutting behind us with a jarring metallic thud. When we reach the interview room, I pause at the threshold. He's already there, shackled at the wrists and ankles, seated on the opposite side of the table. His hair has turned gray, and his skin is pale from months without sunlight. But his eyes, with their manic glint, haven't changed.

"Dr. Carter," he says, his mouth twisting into a creepy smile. "You came to visit an old friend."

I sit down and place my recorder on the table between us. "This isn't a visit. It's an interview. And I'm certainly not your friend, Kosminski."

"Call me Jack," he murmurs, leaning forward just enough for the chains to rattle.

I ignore the bait. "Are you ready for my first question?"

"I don't think it's very fair. I didn't study for the exam."

I sigh and continue. "How many people have you killed?"

He tilts his head, considering, and I notice the tang of stale sweat, the sour edge of unwashed hair. His fingers drum nervously on the table, his hands grimy, his nails blackened, and there are dark circles under his eyes. "Dozens. Perhaps more," he says. "After a while, they start to blur together–faces, places, centuries."

"Centuries?" I shake my head. "Just Rita in this one, correct?"

He shrugs, and a chill goes up my spine. "If you say so."

My pulse increases. "Are you saying you killed more women in New York–or are you implying something else?"

His devious smile grows. "Why would I admit anything to you?"

I press on, my voice calm. "I have a theory that you are Peter Kürten? Or H. H. Holmes?"

He chuckles, a harsh, rattling sound that makes the hair on the back of my neck prickle. His head tilts sharply, jerking to one side, his lips pulling back in a twitching, uneven grin. "No. They were admirers," he says. "I like to think I inspired them. But no, I was never that sloppy."

His gestures are erratic, his muscles stiff, and the way he moves makes him appear untethered, as if he's teetering on the edge of his own world.

"You have no power to jump through time. You just followed me." Each word is measured. I'm daring him to admit something different.

All I get in response is a smile. If he could leap–he would have done so, wouldn't he? Could he escape this prison? Wouldn't he have done so by now?

It's clear he's not going to answer me, so I change my line of questioning. "Why do you hate women?" I ask.

The smile falters. He leans back, the chains clinking softly. "All women are the same. Whores. Bitches. Just like my mother." His eyes glass over, and he's faraway now. "She said my voice was an offense to God. Once, she stabbed my tongue for talking too much." He opens his mouth and sticks out his tongue enough for me to see a pale, puckered scar slicing across the muscle.

For a second, against every instinct, I almost feel sorry for him. Then, I remember what he did to Rita Shaw, to Shannon, and to every other unfortunate woman who crossed his path.

"How did you survive the gunshot in London?" I ask.

He shrugs. "The bullet only grazed me. I fell into the water, and when I woke up, I swam until I reached shore. Someone found me and took me to a hospital. When I was well again, I started looking for you."

The room suddenly feels too small. "How did you get to New York?"

His grin returns, thin and cruel. "It wasn't too difficult for me to find my way. There are others like me, you know? You'd be amazed how little people notice what hides in the shadows and doesn't make any noise."

I force myself not to react to his taunting. "One more question."

He eagerly leans forward again. "Ask me anything, Doc."

"Why Shannon?"

His expression hardens. "Your little red bird was kind to me," he says. "And kindness is weakness." He smiles as if he's proud.

I turn off the recorder, knowing no one can ever hear this conversation or they'll think we're both insane.

My chair screeches across the floor as I push back from the table. "Goodbye, Aaron. Have fun with the other murderers until you find yourself rotting in hell."

His only response is that deep growl of a laugh.

I stare at him for one long moment before I turn on my heel and walk away, refusing to look back.

The prison doors clang shut behind me, and Mark is waiting in the lot, leaning against the car, his hands stuffed in his coat pockets. I look into his eyes, and there's that familiar mix of protectiveness and pride that always makes me feel seen.

"Are you all right?" he asks.

"Better than all right," I say as we get in the car. "He's locked up. The blood, the letters, the threats… it's all over."

Mark starts the car, and we head uptown. Buildings flash by outside of the windows. I lean back in the seat, finally relaxing completely.

"We're still meeting your mother," he says. "But we have a stop to make first."

"Where?" I ask, incredibly intrigued.

He shrugs as if his surprise is nothing, his Victorian politeness layered over a boyish grin. "It's a secret."

I don't usually like secrets. Historically, surprises include being chased through a foggy alley, but this time, I catch myself smiling.

When he turns the car, the towering façade of Rockefeller Center comes into view, its lights twinkling over the plaza and crowds moving like a river below. The Christmas tree soars above everything, a living spire of light that seems too bright to be real. Snowflakes wink at us through beams from the street lamps.

"You brought me to Rockefeller Plaza?" I say while he searches for a parking spot. We finally get lucky and find one only a few blocks over. "I knew you wanted to see it, but I didn't know you wanted to stop here tonight."

Mark turns the engine off. "Do you like it?" he asks.

"Of course I do. I love everything about this place."

We get out of the car and walk over to the Christmas tree hand in hand. I gaze up at the tree above us; its lights twinkle like constellations.

When I turn back to Mark, he's down on one knee. "Lena, from the moment we met, I have known you to be fearless, brilliant, beautiful, strong, kind, and special. Through centuries, through impossibilities, through unbelievable hardship, you remain extraordinary. I can't fathom any future without you by my side. Will you marry me?"

My eyes widen and fill with tears. "Yes," I say instantly, and the crowd around us cheers. Complete strangers clap, and someone whistles.

Through the sparkle and applause, I suddenly notice my mom, beaming with pride, her phone in her hands. She's filmed the proposal, and I'm so thankful for that–and for her.

Mark stands and slides the ring onto my finger. "It's gorgeous." Tears of joy stream down my cheeks. We are triumphant in this moment. Even time itself can't come between us.

He pulls me into his arms and kisses me. The noise of the crowd fades until it's just us, the world passing by while we stand still beneath thousands of lights.

My mom joins us a moment later, her face flushed with cold and happiness. She hugs me tightly, then hugs Mark. When she steps back, she wipes her eyes. "It's about time," she says, laughing through the tears. "I'll leave you two for your first date as an engaged couple, but I'm going to send you the proposal video as soon as I get home."

I hug her once more before she leaves.

Mark takes my hand again, his thumb brushing over the ring, and we walk toward the edge of the plaza. The ice rink glimmers below. A street musician plays "Have Yourself a Merry Little Christmas" on a saxophone, the notes pure and sweet. For a second, New York feels gentle.

Later, when we reach the car, Mark glances up at the sky. The snow is starting to fall harder now. "I used to think time was a curse," he says. "That it was something to outrun. But now, I think it's a gift because it led you to me."

I lean my head on his shoulder. "Let's make the most of it then."

I think about how impossible it all is. A year ago, my life felt like a constant chase, every day shadowed by fear and uncertainty, and now here I am, alive, breathing, and sure that we've made it through.

Mark is with me, and life is no longer about protection or heroics, but instead, it's about being present and sharing a happy and fulfilled life together. I think about every choice that led us here, every risk, every hard decision, and every time we thought we couldn't go on. Each moment mattered. Each moment brought me to this life, to this person, and to this possibility.

I let myself feel the joy, awe, and disbelief. There are no more monsters chasing us, no centuries to run through, and no more terrifying threats. The past shaped us, the future is ours to claim, and this life, exciting and miraculous, stretches out ahead of us.

We are exactly where we need to be. We aren't just surviving anymore.

Now, we are truly *living*, and at last, we are home.

*Thank you for reading!* Back to the Old West *will release January 15, 2026!*

# ALSO BY ID JOHNSON

**Stand Alone Titles**

<u>All I Want for Christmas is Pooch</u>

*(<u>sweet contemporary romance</u>)*

<u>Christmas Memory</u>

*(<u>sweet contemporary romance</u>)*

<u>Meet Cute Me Under the Mistletoe</u>

*(<u>sweet contemporary romance</u>)*

<u>The Doll Maker's Daughter at Christmas</u>

*(clean romance/historical)*

<u>Pretty Little Monster</u>

*(young adult/suspense)*

<u>The Journey to Normal: Our Family's Life with Autism</u> *(nonfiction)*

<u>Found by the Alpha *(fantasy romance)*</u>

**Sweet As Maple Syrup series**

Leaving Autumn

Cold Turkey

Snowed Inn

**Love Throughout Time**

*(time travel romance)*

Back to Titanic (free!)

Back to Gettysburg

Back to Bunker Hill

Back to the Highlands

Back to Port Royal

Back to the Inquisition

Back to Salem

Back to Plymouth

Back to Whitechapel

Back to the Old West (Jan 2026)

Back to the Ton (Feb 2026)

Back to the Crown (March 2026)

Back to Pompeii (April 2026)

**Silverwood Academy**

*(paranormal romance)*

Vampire Hunter (free!)

World Builder

Realm Jumper

**Celestial Springs**

*(psychological thriller/literary fiction/women's fiction)*

Beneath the Inconstant Moon

The First Mrs. Edwards

Leaving Ginny

**The Motherhood**

*(dystopian romance)*

Rain's Rebellion (free!)

Rain's Run

Rain's Return

**Ashes and Rose Petals**

*(contemporary romance/retelling of Romeo and Juliet and Cinderella)*

Girl in the Attic (free!)

Girl From the Tomb

<u>Girl On the Beach</u>

**Nashville Country Dreams**

*(contemporary romance)*

<u>Meant to Marry Me (free!)</u>

<u>Lead Me Home</u>

<u>You Are the Reason</u>

**Forever Love series**

*(clean romance/historical)*

<u>Cordia's Will: A Civil War Story of Love and Loss</u>

<u>Cordia's Hope: A Story of Love on the Frontier</u>

**The Clandestine Saga series**

*(paranormal romance)*

<u>Transformation (free!)</u>

<u>Resurrection</u>

<u>Repercussion</u>

<u>Absolution</u>

<u>Illumination</u>

<u>Destruction</u>

<u>Annihilation</u>

<u>Obliteration</u>

<u>Termination</u>

**A Vampire Hunter's Tale (based on The Clandestine Saga)**

*(paranormal/alternate history)*

<u>Aaron (free!)</u>

<u>Jamie</u>

<u>Elliott</u>

<u>Christian</u>

**The Chronicles of Cassidy (based on The Clandestine Saga)**

*(young adult paranormal)*

So You Think Your Sister's a Vampire Hunter? (free!)

Who Wants to Be a Vampire Hunter?

How Not to Be a Vampire Hunter

My Life As a Teenage Vampire Hunter

Vampire Hunting Isn't for Morons

Vampires Bite and Other Life Lessons

Gone Guardian

Death Does Not Become Her


**Blood of the Vampire Hunter (based on The Clandestine Saga)**

*(paranormal romance)*

Night Slayer (free!)

Shadow Stalker

Queen Catcher

Mother Hunter

Father Finder


**Ghosts of Southampton series**

*(historical romance)*

Prelude

Titanic

Residuum

Lusitania


**Heartwarming Holidays Sweet Romance series**

*(Christian/clean romance)*

Melody's Christmas (free!)

Christmas Cocoa

Winter Woods

<u>Waiting On Love</u>

<u>Shamrock Hearts</u>

<u>A Blossoming Spring Romance</u>

<u>Firecracker!</u>

<u>Falling in Love</u>

<u>Thankful for You</u>

<u>Melody's Christmas Wedding</u>

<u>The New Year's Date</u>

**Charles Town Brides (based on Heartwarming Holidays Sweet Romance)**

*(Christian/clean romance)*

<u>From This Moment (free!)</u>

<u>Can't Help Falling in Love</u>

<u>It's Your Love</u>

<u>When You Say Nothing At All</u>

<u>My Girl</u>

<u>Unchained Melody</u>

<u>I Only Have Eyes For You</u>

<u>At Last</u>

<u>The Very Thought of You</u>

**Reaper's Hollow**

*(paranormal/urban fantasy)*

<u>Ruin's Lot (free!)</u>

<u>Ruin's Promise</u>

<u>Ruin's Legacy</u>

**When Kings Collide**

*(steamy historical romance)*

<u>Princess of Silence</u>

<u>Princess of Hearts</u>

**Collections**
<u>Ghosts of Southampton Books 0-2</u>
<u>Reaper's Hollow Books 1-3</u>
<u>The Clandestine Saga Books 1-3</u>
<u>The Chronicles of Cassidy Books 1-4</u>
<u>Celestial Springs Collection</u>
<u>Heartwarming Holidays Sweet Romance Books 1-3</u>
<u>Heartwarming Holidays Sweet Romance Books 4-7</u>

Websites: https://idjohnsonwriter.com/

Follow us on TikTok: @roguewolfpublishing

Follow on Twitter @authoridjohnson

Find me on Facebook at <u>www.facebook.com/IDJohnsonAuthor</u>

Instagram: @authoridjohnson

Follow me on Bookbub: https://www.bookbub.com/authors/id-johnson